D. H. Lawrence

The Rocking-Horse Winner

Edited by
Dominick P. Consolo
Denison University

The Merrill Literary Casebook Series
Edward P.J. Corbett, Editor

Charles E. Merrill Publishing Company
A Bell & Howell Company
Columbus, Ohio

W9-DDD-731

56767

4-91

Standard Book Number: 675-09445-3

Library of Congress Catalog Number: 76-92599

1 2 3 4 5 6 7 8 9 10—73 72 71 70 69

Printed in the United States of America

Foreword

The Charles E. Merrill Literary Casebook Series deals with short literary works, arbitrarily defined here as "works which can be easily read in a single sitting." Accordingly, the series will concentrate on poems, short stories, brief dramas, and literary essays. These casebooks are designed to be used in literature courses or in practical criticism courses where the instructor wants to expose his students to an extensive and intensive study of a single, short work or in composition courses where the instructor wants to expose his students to the discipline of writing a research paper on a literary text.

All of the casebooks in the series follow this format: (1) foreword; (2) general instructions for the writing of a research paper; (3) the editor's Introduction; (4) the text of the literary work; (5) a number of critical articles on the literary work; (6) suggested topics for short papers on the literary work; (7) suggested topics for long (10-15 pages) papers on the literary work; (8) a selective bibliography of additional readings on the literary work. Some of the casebooks, especially those dealing with poetry, may carry an additional section, which contains such features as variant versions of the work, a closely related literary work, comments by the author and his contemporaries on the work.

So that students might simulate first-hand research in library copies of books and bound periodicals, each of the critical articles carries full bibliographical information at the bottom of the first page of the article, and the text of the article carries the actual page-numbers of the original source. A notation like /131/ after a word in the text indicates that *after* that word in the original source the article went over to page 131. All of the text between that number and the next number, /132/, can be taken as occurring on page 131 of the original source.

Edward P.J. Corbett
General Editor

Contents

Introduction   1

Chronology of Significant Dates   6

The Rocking-Horse Winner by D. H. Lawrence   9

Harry T. Moore, *Some Notes on "The Rocking-Horse Winner"*   23

W. D. Snodgrass, *A Rocking-Horse: The Symbol, the Pattern, the Way to Live*   26

Carolyn Gordon and Allen Tate, *Commentary on "The Rocking-Horse Winner"*   37

Robert Gorham Davis, *Observations on "The Rocking-Horse Winner"*   41

Kingsley Widmer, *The Triumph of the Middleclass Matriarch*   43

Roy Lamson, Hallett Smith, Hugh Maclean, Wallace W. Douglas, *A Critical Analysis*   47

W. R. Martin, *Fancy or Imagination? "The Rocking-Horse Winner"*   52

William D. Burroughs, *No Defense for "The Rocking-Horse Winner"*   55

Robert G. Lawrence, *Further Notes on D. H. Lawrence's Rocking-Horse*   57

Frank O'Connor, *Poe and "The Rocking-Horse Winner"*   58

James G. Hepburn, *Disarming and Uncanny Visions*   60

E. W. Tedlock, Jr., *Values and "The Rocking-Horse Winner"*   69

W. S. Marks III, *The Psychology of the Uncanny in Lawrence's "The Rocking-Horse Winner"*   71

Frank Amon, *D. H. Lawrence and the Short Story*   84

Frederick W. Turner III, *Prancing in to a Purpose: Myths,*
    Horses, and True Selfhood in Lawrence's "The
    Rocking-Horse Winner"   95

Suggestions for Papers   107

Additional Readings   109

Glossary   111

General Instructions For A Research Paper   115

Introduction

His mother had fondly called him "Bertie"; his wife Frieda called him "Lawrence." Some of the complexity of the man (and artist) may be suggested in the polarity of the two names—the one diminutive and affectionate, the other almost formal, yet casually grand. Polarities may, in fact, be the only way one can approximate the truth of this writer of much transcendent sense and some nonsense, who is capable of moving us with that insistence of genius. Consider the polarity of his growing years, when, weak and frail as a child, he was sensitive both to the harsh idiom of his hard-working, hard-drinking father, a miner of coal, and to the warm persuasion of his ex-schoolteacher mother, a sometime poet and believer in the "one narrow way of salvation ('the *blood* of the Lamb')."[1] The pull between the two is powerfully rendered in the adolescent experiences of Paul Morel in Lawrence's first major novel, *Sons and Lovers.* Apparently like his fictional counterpart in this most "autobiographical" of his novels, Lawrence responded to his father with a kind of love-hate. To his mother, he responded with deep affection. Mrs. Lawrence was possessive and ambitious for her children. After the death of her oldest son, she made "Bertie" her favorite. It was not until her own death in 1910, when he was twenty-five, that Lawrence could, and did, become formally engaged to the beautiful Louie Burrows. The engagement dragged on for some fifteen months. Lawrence's health deteriorated, forcing him to give up his teaching in Croyden, but he continued to labor away on the novel he would later call *Sons and Lovers.* The engagement came to a shocking conclusion in May 1912, when Lawrence went off to Germany with the wife of a Nottingham professor and the mother of three, Frieda Weekley (née Von Richthofen).

Intelligent, well-read, talkative, warm, and passionate, Frieda contributed significantly to Lawrence's development and maturity as an artist. Opinions differ, however, as to the extent and the kind of

---

[1] Kenneth Young, *D. H. Lawrence* (London, 1952), p. 16

1

influence Frieda exerted on Lawrence. The most intriguing argument
is whether Frieda instructed Lawrence in the new psychology of
Freud, particularly the "Oedipus-complex," hailed by reviewers as
the dramatic center of *Sons and Lovers*.[2] In retrospect, the question is
largely academic. Frieda's influence was and continued to be that
of *woman*, the opposite to Lawrence as *male*, a relationship which,
Lawrence believed, resulted in a creative tension. I may be guilty of
some mythicizing here and may perhaps warrant Lawrence's own
rebuke to Frieda, whom he once told to "stop talking like a character
from one" of his own novels. Yet each brought to their relationship
a Singleness of Being and it was the experience of their intimate life,
I am convinced, that led Lawrence in his fiction to affirm polarity as a
dynamic principle. This is the unity-in-duality he dramatized in *The
Rainbow*, and theorized as "star-equilibrium" in *Women in Love*.
The point to be made about Frieda, emerging quite clearly from
accounts of their warm and tempestuous relationships in England, on
the Continent, in New Mexico, is that she was equal to Lawrence's
needs both as a man and as an artist. Indeed, she was the very antithesis of the life-denying, loveless women in his novels and stories.

Of those loveless women, Paul's mother in "The Rocking-Horse
Winner" will be my main concern here. My hope in considering the
mother's role in that story is to extend by a little the judicious range
of critical opinion in this collection. In doing so I forego happily an
abstract of what each essay has to offer, leaving that discovery to the
reader. I forego also what would be at best a brief and skeletal account of Lawrence's life, relegating essential matter and dates to a
simple biographical chronology.

It was the film version of "The Rocking-Horse Winner" that first
fixed my interest in the story.[3] Still etched in memory is the frighten-
ing, awesome tableau of the dramatic climax when the boy's mother
opens the door to Paul's room and snaps on the light, revealing his
charging form at the moment he has "got there" to learn the name of
his final winner. Powerful in effect as that moment was (caught with
all the striking immediacy of cinematic resources), its complex of
meaning, including the apparent unenlightenment of the mother, can
only be discovered in a close reading of the story itself. Once then

---

[2] It is interesting here to draw one's own conclusions by reading first-hand accounts
by Frieda Lawrence and first "love" Jessie Chambers in their respective books
(listed in the additional readings).

[3] See p. 279 from Harry T. Moore's *The Life and Works of D. H. Lawrence* for the
names of the cast, scenarist, and director. A brief review of the film is included by
Pauline Kael in *Kiss Kiss Bang Bang* (Little, Brown and Company, 1968).

learns that the moment brings together two dominant images—of eyes and of hardening—that can be traced in intensifying lines from the story's beginning to the climax. Initially, these images underscore the tension between the mother Hester and her children; progressively, they register the widening gulf between herself and Paul, mother and son. At the climax of the story, they serve to intensify the final effects of lovelessness and misplaced values. But further, and of importance, they offer us another *perspective* of Hester. In being alert to these images, the reader also becomes aware of the harmony in this story between technique and substance, style and content. The style embodies meaning here as completely and successfully as in Lawrence's greatest novel, *Women in Love,* published four years before in 1921. The story, in fact, shares common elements with it. "In point of style," Lawrence wrote in the Foreword to that novel, "fault is often found with the continual, slightly modified repetition. The only answer is that it is natural to the author; and that every natural crisis in emotion or passion or understanding comes from this pulsing, frictional to-and-fro which works up to culmination."

The sexual metaphor that Lawrence uses with deliberate intent carries obvious stylistic and thematic implications for that novel. In addition, it supplies as well a description of the style of "The Rocking-Horse Winner." Other affinities in point of style are not with prose fiction but with the traditional English ballad, specifically with its incremental repetition and incantatory effect. This effect is abetted in the story by the seemingly impartial omniscient narrator to whom we quite readily surrender our disbelief. The simple monosyllabic language with which he informs us of the situation in the opening paragraph does not admit of incredulity. Unobtrusively, all the key terms to be repeated simply or with slight variation are introduced: "luck," "love," "dust," "felt," "knew," and "anxious." The images are established: how the center of the mother's heart goes "hard"; and how the children reflect this knowledge in each other's "eyes." Only "money" receives no attention in the first paragraph, but since the word is shortly to be mentioned, its association with the key terms will be immediate and relevant; the need for more money creates "anxiety" in the house, "lucre" will be confused with "luck," and both will be interrelated as a substitute for "love."

Critics have often remarked on the peculiar power of the story's opening, yet it remains to be pointed out that the effect is due to the simplicity of the informative statements: the situation is "given" to us in a tone so unassuming that we neither question the truth of its psychology nor judge the woman.

There was woman who was beautiful, who started with all the advantages, yet she had no luck. She married for love, and the love turned to dust. She had bonny children, yet she felt they had been thrust upon her, and she could not love them.

That third sentence is one of sheer genius in its suggestive power, not alone for what Snodgrass in his article points out are the implications of the verb "thrust"—and they are many. Lawrence establishes what he will stress throughout by repetition, an interplay between statement and image that gets logically at the effects of misplaced values. The opening statement tells us that she cannot feel love; the image shortly to follow (that at the "centre" of her heart there was a "hard place") will tell us she can *feel*: anxiety, reproach, the need to "cover up some fault." The image itself, by suggesting an *absence* of feeling, creates a fine irony, for Hester's condition is infinitely worse—a negativity, which like the whispers of the house, grows by what it feeds upon, an appetite never to be appeased.

While the mother becomes almost depersonalized by her obsession with money, the house and its inanimate objects, conversely, come alive, reacting to the unspoken phrase, "There must be more money." The quickened house silences the children. Their knowledge of the phrase is mirrored in their "eyes." When Paul questions his mother about luck, which she defines, concluding that if "you're lucky, you will always get more money," Paul looks at her with "unsure eyes." What she does not realize is that her definition—"what causes you to have money"—establishes the conditions by which Paul can measure, be "sure," prove himself. But since the terms are those of an impossible fulfillment, "always get more money," he will have to expend all his vitality, burn himself up in getting there.

Beginning to search inwardly for luck, knowing he can get there on his rocking-horse, Paul's eyes for the first time take on a "strange glare." From this moment on, until he loses consciousness in his mother's arms, the image of the glare is insisted upon and repeated with variations—"blue glare," "hot-blue eyes," "blue fire"—some thirteen times. The effect is one of fearful anticipation as the subtle implications of the images, interacting with the key terms, carry us inexorably forward to the recognition scene and the story's climax:

His eyes *blazed* at her for one strange and senseless second, as he ceased urging his wooden horse. Then he fell with a crash to the ground, and she, all her tormented motherhood *flooding* upon her, rushed to gather him up. (Emphases mine.)

What is so terribly moving here is the cumulative power of the repeated image of the eyes now "blaz[ing]" and, as it were, "flooding" the mother with intense light. It is at once a blaze of triumph and of accusation and condemnation. Paul got there, proving that he *was* lucky, but at a cost, the image suggests, of almost literal self-consumption.

Yet there is another aspect to this moment which a consideration of the second dominating image, that of Hester's "hardening" and "cold" heart, makes clear. This image, too, follows an intensifying line as it is repeated with variations—"centre . . . go hard," "hard little place," "heart curiously heavy"—until in the final scene her "heart stood still" and she is "frozen" with anxiety and fear. The culmination of this image suggests that another meaning, one of irony and pathos that tempers the condemnation, is also implied in the "flooding": Hester's heart has finally responded to Paul's fire, and thawed. Her being for the first time is inundated by a genuine concern.

Thus when the image, "heart-frozen," appears once more, its association is with her fear and concern for her son. She has had her illumination, yet we know that it has come too late. So, in a final use of the images, both merged significantly into one—Paul's eyes becoming "like two stones," and his mother's heart turning "actually into a stone." When the light goes out of his eyes, the very life goes out of her heart. It is Bassett, that perverse "hound of heaven,"[4] whose eyes will "glitter." Uncle Oscar will soothe: "My God, Hester, you're eighty-odd thousand to the good," but it is we, who, made aware of Hester's pain of loss, know the stoic understatement of her "No, you never did" when set against Paul's last words: "Mother, did I ever tell you? I *am* lucky."

---

[4]See the last entry in the Suggestions for Short Papers.

Chronology of Significant Dates

1885 Lawrence born, Eastwood, Nottinghamshire to a collier and his ex-schoolteacher wife.

1901 Works for surgical appliance maker after leaving high school; meets Jessie Chambers.

1902 Seriously ill with pulmonary infection; nursed through by mother.

1903 Studies at Nottingham College; teaches at British School, Eastwood.

1909 Publishes poems in *The English Review*.

1910 Mother dies after painful illness.

1911 First novel, *The White Peacock*.

1912 Meets Frieda Weekley, married and mother of three. They go off together to Germany.

1913 Publishes *Sons And Lovers*.

1914 Marries Frieda in England.

1915 Brief intense friendship with Bertrand Russell; *The Rainbow* published.

1917 Suspected of spying; ordered to leave Cornwall.

1919 To Italy and beginnings of years of travel.

1920 Publishes *Women In Love*.

1922 To Ceylon and Australia. In September to New Mexico. Publishes *Fantasia of the Unconscious*. Previous year published *Psychoanalysis of the Unconscious*.

1923 Publishes *Studies in Classic American Literature*. Frieda leaves Lawrence in New York and returns to England.

1925 Together with Frieda in New Mexico. Publishes *St. Mawr, Reflections on the Death of a Porcupine*; "The Rocking-Horse Winner." Seriously ill.

1926 Publishes *The Plumed Serpent.*

1928 Publishes *Lady Chatterley's Lover* by subscription.

1929 Exhibition of paintings in London; a number seized, threatened with destruction.

1930 Dies in March at Vence, France, of tuberculosis.

The Rocking-Horse Winner*

There was a woman who was beautiful, who started with all the advantages, yet she had no luck. She married for love, and the love turned to dust. She had bonny children, yet she felt they had been thrust upon her, and she could not love them. They looked at her coldly, as if they were finding fault with her. And hurriedly she felt she must cover up some fault in herself. Yet what it was that she must cover up she never knew. Nevertheless, when her children were present, she always felt the centre of her heart go hard. This troubled her, and in her manner she was all the more gentle and anxious for her children, as if she loved them very much. Only she herself knew that at the centre of her heart was a hard little place that could not feel love, no, not for anybody. Everybody else said of her: "She is such a good mother. She adores her children." Only she herself, and her children themselves, knew it was not so. They read it in each other's eyes.

There were a boy and two little girls. They lived in a pleasant house, with a garden, and they had discreet servants, and felt themselves superior to anyone in the neighbourhood.

Although they lived in style, they felt always an anxiety in the house. There was never enough money. The mother had a small income, and the father had a small income, but not nearly enough for the social position which they had to keep up. The father went into town to some office. But though he had good prospects, these prospects never materialised. There was always the grinding sense of the shortage of money, though the style was always kept up.

At last the mother said: "I will see if *I* can't make something." But she did not know where to begin. She racked her brains, and tried this thing and the other, but could not find anything successful. The failure made deep lines come into her face. Her children were growing

*Reprinted from *The Complete Short Stories of D. H. Lawrence*, Vol. III. Copyright 1933 by the Estate of D. H. Lawrence, © 1961 by Angelo Ravagli and C. Montague Weekley, executors of the Estate of Frieda Lawrence Ravagli. Reprinted by permission of the Viking Press, Inc.

up, they would have to go to school. There must be more money, there must be more money. The father, who was always very handsome and expensive in his tastes, seemed as if he never *would* be able to do anything worth doing. And the mother, who had a great belief in herself, did not succeed any better, and her tastes were just as expensive.

And so the house came to be haunted by the unspoken phrase: *There must be more money! There must be more money!* The children could hear it all the time, though nobody said it aloud. They heard it at Christmas, when the expensive and splendid toys filled the nursery. Behind the shining modern rocking-horse, behind the smart doll's house, a voice would start whispering: "There *must* be more money! There *must* be more money!" And the children would stop playing, to listen for a moment. They would look into each other's eyes, to see if they had all heard. And each one saw in the eyes of the other two that they too had heard. "There *must* be more money! There *must* be more money!"

It came whispering from the springs of the still-swaying rocking-horse, and even the horse, bending his wooden, champing head, heard it. The big doll, sitting so pink and smirking in her new pram, could hear it quite plainly, and seemed to be smirking all the more self-consciously because of it. The foolish puppy, too, that took the place of the teddybear, he was looking so extraordinarily foolish for no other reason but that he heard the secret whisper all over the house: "There *must* be more money!"

Yet nobody ever said it aloud. The whisper was everywhere, and therefore no one spoke it. Just as no one ever says: "We are breathing!" in spite of the fact that breath is coming and going all the time.

"Mother," said the boy Paul one day, "why don't we keep a car of our own? Why do we always use uncle's, or else a taxi?"

"Because we're the poor members of the family," said the mother.

"But why *are* we, mother?"

"Well — I suppose," she said slowly and bitterly, "it's because your father has no luck."

The boy was silent for some time.

"Is luck money, mother?" he asked, rather timidly.

"No, Paul. Not quite. It's what causes you to have money."

"Oh!" said Paul vaguely. "I thought when Uncle Oscar said *filthy lucker*, it meant money."

"*Filthy lucre* does mean money," said the mother. "But it's lucre, not luck."

"Oh!" said the boy. "Then what *is* luck, mother?"

"It's what causes you to have money. If you're lucky you have money. That's why it's better to be born lucky than rich. If you're rich, you may lose your money. But if you're lucky, you will always get more money."

"Oh! Will you? And is father not lucky?"

"Very unlucky, I should say," she said bitterly.

The boy watched her with unsure eyes.

"Why?" he asked.

"I don't know. Nobody ever knows why one person is lucky and another unlucky."

"Don't they? Nobody at all? Does *nobody* know?"

"Perhaps God. But He never tells."

"He ought to, then. And aren't you lucky either, mother?"

"I can't be, if I married an unlucky husband."

"But by yourself, aren't you?"

"I used to think I was, before I married. Now I think I am very unlucky indeed."

"Why?"

"Well — never mind! Perhaps I'm not really," she said.

The child looked at her to see if she meant it. But he saw, by the lines of her mouth, that she was only trying to hide something from him.

"Well, anyhow," he said stoutly, "I'm a lucky person."

"Why?" said his mother, with a sudden laugh.

He stared at her. He didn't even know why he had said it.

"God told me," he asserted, brazening it out.

"I hope He did, dear!" she said, again with a laugh, but rather bitter.

"He did, mother!"

"Excellent!" said the mother, using one of her husband's exclamations.

The boy saw she did not believe him; or rather, that she paid no attention to his assertion. This angered him somewhere, and made him want to compel her attention.

He went off by himself, vaguely, in a childish way, seeking for the clue to 'luck'. Absorbed, taking no heed of other people, he went about with a sort of stealth, seeking inwardly for luck. He wanted luck, he wanted it, he wanted it. When the two girls were playing dolls in the nursery, he would sit on his big rocking-horse, charging madly into space, with a frenzy that made the little girls peer at him uneasily. Wildly the horse careered, the waving dark hair of the body tossed, his eyes had a strange glare in them. The little girls dared not speak to him.

When he had ridden to the end of his mad little journey, he climbed down and stood in front of his rocking-horse, staring fixedly into its lowered face. Its red mouth was slightly open, its big eye was wide and glassy-bright.

"Now!" he would silently command the snorting steed. "Now, take me to where there is luck! Now take me!"

And he would slash the horse on the neck with the little whip he had asked Uncle Oscar for. He *knew* the horse could take him to where there was luck, if only he forced it. So he would mount again and start on his furious ride, hoping at last to get there. He knew he could get there.

"You'll break your horse, Paul!" said the nurse.

"He's always riding like that! I wish he'd leave off!" said his elder sister Joan.

But he only glared down on them in silence. Nurse gave him up. She could make nothing of him. Anyhow, he was growing beyond her.

One day his mother and his Uncle Oscar came in when he was on one of his furious rides. He did not speak to them.

"Hallo, you young jockey! Riding a winner?" said his uncle.

"Aren't you growing too big for a rocking-horse? You're not a very little boy any longer, you know," said his mother.

But Paul only gave a blue glare from his big, rather close-set eyes. He would speak to nobody when he was in full tilt. His mother watched him with an anxious expression on her face.

At last he suddenly stopped forcing his horse into the mechanical gallop and slid down.

"Well, I got there!" he announced fiercely, his blue eyes still flaring, and his sturdy long legs straddling apart.

"Where did you get to?" asked his mother.

"Where I wanted to go," he flared back at her.

"That's right son!" said Uncle Oscar. "Don't you stop till you get there. What's the horse's name?"

"He doesn't have a name," said the boy.

"Gets on without all right?" asked the uncle.

"Well, he has different names. He was called Sansovino last week."

"Sansovino, eh? Won the Ascot. How did you know this name?"

"He always talks about horse-races with Bassett," said Joan.

The uncle was delighted to find that his small nephew was posted with all the racing news. Bassett, the young gardener, who had been wounded in the left foot in the war and had got his present job through Oscar Cresswell, whose batman he had been, was a perfect blade of the 'turf'. He lived in the racing events, and the small boy lived with him.

Oscar Cresswell got it all from Bassett.

"Master Paul comes and asks me, so I can't do more than tell him, sir," said Bassett, his face terribly serious, as if he were speaking of religious matters.

"And does he ever put anything on a horse he fancies?"

"Well — I don't want to give him away — he's a young sport, a fine sport, sir. Would you mind asking him himself? He sort of takes a pleasure in it, and perhaps he'd feel I was giving him away, sir, if you don't mind."

Bassett was serious as a church.

The uncle went back to his nephew and took him off for a ride in the car.

"Say, Paul, old man, do you ever put anything on a horse?" the uncle asked.

The boy watched the handsome man closely.

"Why, do you think I oughtn't to?" he parried.

"Not a bit of it! I thought perhaps you might give me a tip for the Lincoln."

The car sped on into the country, going down to Uncle Oscar's place in Hampshire.

"Honour bright?" said the nephew.

"Honour bright, son!" said the uncle.

"Well, then, Daffodil."

"Daffodil! I doubt it, sonny. What about Mirza?"

"I only know the winner," said the boy. "That's Daffodil."

"Daffodil, eh?"

There was a pause. Daffodil was an obscure horse comparatively.

"Uncle!"

"Yes, son?"

"You won't let it go any further, will you? I promised Bassett."

"Bassett be damned, old man! What's he got to do with it?"

"We're partners. We've been partners from the first. Uncle, he lent me my first five shillings, which I lost. I promised him, honour bright, it was only between me and him; only you gave me that ten-shilling note I started winning with, so I thought you were lucky. You won't let it go any further, will you?"

The boy gazed at his uncle from those big, hot, blue eyes, set rather close together. The uncle stirred and laughed uneasily.

"Right you are, son! I'll keep your tip private. Daffodil, eh? How much are you putting on him?"

"All except twenty pounds," said the boy. "I keep that in reserve."

The uncle thought it a good joke.

"You keep twenty pounds in reserve, do you, you young romancer? What are you betting, then?"

"I'm betting three hundred," said the boy gravely. "But it's between you and me, Uncle Oscar! Honour bright?"

The uncle burst into a roar of laughter.

"It's between you and me all right, you young Nat Gould," he said, laughing. "But where's your three hundred?"

"Bassett keeps it for me. We're partners."

"You are, are you! And what is Bassett putting on Daffodil?"

"He won't go quite as high as I do, I expect. Perhaps he'll go a hundred and fifty."

"What, pennies?" laughed the uncle.

"Pounds," said the child, with a surprised look at his uncle. "Bassett keeps a bigger reserve than I do."

Between wonder and amusement Uncle Oscar was silent. He pursued the matter no further, but he determined to take his nephew with him to the Lincoln races.

"Now, son," he said, "I'm putting twenty on Mirza, and I'll put five on for you on any horse you fancy. What's your pick?"

"Daffodil, uncle."

"No, not the fiver on Daffodil!"

"I should if it was my own fiver," said the child.

"Good! Good! Right you are! A fiver for me and a fiver for you on Daffodil."

The child had never been to a race-meeting before, and his eyes were blue fire. He pursed his mouth tight and watched. A Frenchman just in front had put his money on Lancelot. Wild with excitement, he flayed his arms up and down, yelling *"Lancelot! Lancelot!"* in his French accent.

Daffodil came in first, Lancelot second, Mirza third. The child, flushed and with eyes blazing, was curiously serene. His uncle brought him four five-pound notes, four to one.

"What am I to do with these?" he cried, waving them before the boy's eyes.

"I suppose we'll talk to Bassett," said the boy. "I expect I have fifteen hundred now; and twenty in reserve; and this twenty."

His uncle studied him for some moments.

"Look here, son!" he said. "You're not serious about Bassett and that fifteen hundred, are you?"

"Yes, I am. But it's between you and me, uncle. Honour bright?"

"Honour bright all right, son! But I must talk to Bassett."

"If you'd like to be a partner, uncle, with Bassett and me, we could all be partners. Only, you'd have to promise, honour bright, uncle, not to let it go beyond us three. Bassett and I are lucky, and you must be lucky, because it was your ten shillings I started winning with...."

Uncle Oscar took both Bassett and Paul into Richmond Park for an afternoon, and there they talked.

"It's like this, you see, sir," Bassett said. "Master Paul would get me talking about racing events, spinning yarns, you know, sir. And he was always keen on knowing if I'd made or if I'd lost. It's about a year since, now, that I put five shillings on Blush of Dawn for him: and we lost. Then the luck turned, with that ten shillings he had from you: that we put on Singhalese. And since that time, it's been pretty steady, all things considering. What do you say, Master Paul?"

"We're all right when we're sure," said Paul. "It's when we're not quite sure that we go down."

"Oh, but we're careful then," said Bassett.

"But when are you *sure?*" smiled Uncle Oscar.

"It's Master Paul, sir," said Bassett in a secret, religious voice. "It's as if he had it from heaven. Like Daffodil, now, for the Lincoln. That was as sure as eggs."

"Did you put anything on Daffodil?" asked Oscar Cresswell.

"Yes, sir. I made my bit."

"And my nephew?"

Bassett was obstinately silent, looking at Paul.

"I made twelve hundred, didn't I, Bassett? I told uncle I was putting three hundred on Daffodil."

"That's right," said Bassett, nodding.

"But where's the money?" asked the uncle.

"I keep it safe locked up, sir. Master Paul he can have it any minute he likes to ask for it."

"What, fifteen hundred pounds?"

"And twenty! And *forty*, that is, with the twenty he made on the course."

"It's amazing!" said the uncle.

"If Master Paul offers you to be partners, sir, I would, if I were you: if you'll excuse me," said Bassett.

Oscar Cresswell thought about it.

"I'll see the money," he said.

They drove home again, and, sure enough, Bassett came round to the garden-house with fifteen hundred pounds in notes. The twenty pounds reserve was left with Joe Glee, in the Turf Commission deposit.

"You see, it's all right, uncle, when I'm *sure!* Then we go strong, for all we're worth. Don't we, Bassett?"

"We do that, Master Paul."

"And when are you sure?" said the uncle, laughing.

"Oh, well, sometimes I'm *absolutely* sure, like about Daffodil," said the boy; "and sometimes I have an idea; and sometimes I haven't even an idea, have I, Bassett? Then we're careful, because we mostly go down."

"You do, do you! And when you're sure, like about Daffodil, what makes you sure, sonny?"

"Oh, well, I don't know," said the boy uneasily. "I'm sure, you know, uncle; that's all."

"It's as if he had it from heaven, sir," Bassett reiterated.

"I should say so!" said the uncle.

But he became a partner. And when the Leger was coming on Paul was 'sure' about Lively Spark, which was a quite inconsiderable horse. The boy insisted on putting a thousand on the horse, Bassett went for five hundred, and Oscar Cresswell two hundred. Lively Spark came in first, and the betting had been ten to one against him. Paul had made ten thousand.

"You see," he said, "I was absolutely sure of him."

Even Oscar Cresswell had cleared two thousand.

"Look here, son," he said, "this sort of thing makes me nervous."

"It needn't, uncle! Perhaps I shan't be sure again for a long time."

"But what are you going to do with your money?" asked the uncle.

"Of course," said the boy, "I started it for mother. She said she had no luck, because father is unlucky, so I thought if *I* was lucky, it might stop whispering."

"What might stop whispering?"

"Our house. I *hate* our house for whispering."

"What does it whisper?"

"Why — why" — the boy fidgeted — "why, I don't know. But it's always short of money, you know, uncle."

"I know it, son, I know it."

"You know people send mother writs, don't you, uncle?"

"I'm afraid I do," said the uncle.

"And then the house whispers, like people laughing at you behind your back. It's awful, that is! I thought if I was lucky — "

"You might stop it," added the uncle.

The boy watched him with big blue eyes, that had an uncanny cold fire in them, and he said never a word.

"Well, then!" said the uncle. "What are we doing?"

"I shouldn't like mother to know I was lucky," said the boy.

"Why not, son?"

"She'd stop me."

"I don't think she would."

"Oh!" — and the boy writhed in an odd way — "I *don't* want her to know, uncle."

"All right son! We'll manage it without her knowing."

They managed it very easily. Paul, at the other's suggestion, handed over five thousand pounds to his uncle, who deposited it with the family lawyer, who was then to inform Paul's mother that a relative had put five thousand pounds into his hands, which sum was to be paid out a thousand pounds at a time, on the mother's birthday, for the next five years.

"So she'll have a birthday present of a thousand pounds for five successive years," said Uncle Oscar. "I hope it won't make it all the harder for her later."

Paul's mother had her birthday in November. The house had been 'whispering' worse than ever lately, and, even in spite of his luck, Paul could not bear up against it. He was very anxious to see the effect of the birthday letter, telling his mother about the thousand pounds.

When there were no visitors, Paul now took his meals with his parents, as he was beyond the nursery control. His mother went into town nearly every day. She had discovered that she had an odd knack of sketching furs and dress materials, so she worked secretly in the studio of a friend who was the chief 'artist' for the leading drapers. She drew the figures of ladies in furs and ladies in silk and sequins for the newspaper advertisements. This young woman artist earned several thousand pounds a year, but Paul's mother only made several hundreds, and she was again dissatisfied. She so wanted to be first in something, and she did not succeed, even in making sketches for drapery advertisements.

She was down to breakfast on the morning of her birthday. Paul watched her face as she read her letters. He knew the lawyer's letter. As his mother read it, her face hardened and became more expressionless. Then a cold, determined look came on her mouth. She hid the letter under the pile of others, and said not a word about it.

"Didn't you have anything nice in the post for your birthday, mother?" said Paul.

"Quite moderately nice," she said, her voice cold and absent.

She went away to town without saying more.

But in the afternoon Uncle Oscar appeared. He said Paul's mother had had a long interview with the lawyer, asking if the whole five thousand could not be advanced at once, as she was in debt.

"What do you think, uncle?" said the boy.

"I leave it to you, son."

"Oh, let her have it, then! We can get some more with the other," said the boy.

"A bird in the hand is worth two in the bush, laddie!" said Uncle Oscar.

"But I'm sure to *know* for the Grand National; or the Lincolnshire; or else the Derby. I'm sure to know for *one* of them," said Paul.

So Uncle Oscar signed the agreement, and Paul's mother touched the whole five thousand. Then something very curious happened. The voices in the house suddenly went mad, like a chorus of frogs on a spring evening. There were certain new furnishings, and Paul had a tutor. He was *really* going to Eton, his father's school, in the following autumn. There were flowers in the winter, and a blossoming of the luxury Paul's mother had been used to. And yet the voices in the house, behind the sprays of mimosa and almond-blossom, and from under the piles of iridescent cushions, simply trilled and screamed in a sort of ecstasy: "There *must* be more money! Oh-h-h; there *must* be more money. Oh, now, now-w! Now-w-w — there *must* be more money! — more than ever! More than ever!"

It frightened Paul terribly. He studied away at his Latin and Greek with his tutor. But his intense hours were spent with Bassett. The Grand National had gone by: he had not 'known', and had lost a hundred pounds. Summer was at hand. He was in agony for the Lincoln. But even for the Lincoln he didn't 'know', and he lost fifty pounds. He became wild-eyed and strange, as if something were going to explode in him.

"Let it alone, son! Don't you bother about it!" urged Uncle Oscar. But it was as if the boy couldn't really hear what his uncle was saying.

"I've got to know for the Derby!" the child reiterated, his big blue eyes blazing with a sort of madness.

His mother noticed how overwrought he was.

"You better go to the seaside. Wouldn't you like to go now to the seaside, instead of waiting? I think you'd better," she said, looking down at him anxiously, her heart curiously heavy because of him.

But the child lifted his uncanny blue eyes.

"I couldn't possibly go before the Derby, mother!" he said. "I couldn't possibly!"

"Why not?" she said, her voice becoming heavy when she was opposed. "Why not? You can still go from the seaside to see the Derby with your Uncle Oscar, if that's what you wish. No need for you to wait here. Besides, I think you care too much about these races. It's a bad sign. My family has been a gambling family, and you won't know till you grow up how much damage it has done. But it has done damage. I shall have to send Bassett away, and ask Uncle Oscar not to talk racing to you, unless you promise to be reasonable about it: go away to the seaside and forget it. You're all nerves!"

"I'll do what you like, mother, so long as you don't send me away till after the Derby," the boy said.

"Send you away from where? Just from this house?"

"Yes," he said, gazing at her.

"Why, you curious child, what makes you care about this house so much, suddenly? I never knew you loved it."

He gazed at her without speaking. He had a secret within a secret, something he had not divulged, even to Bassett or to his Uncle Oscar.

But his mother, after standing undecided and a little bit sullen for some moments, said:

"Very well, then! Don't go to the seaside till after the Derby, if you don't wish it. But promise me you won't let your nerves go to pieces. Promise you won't think so much about horse-racing and *events*, as you call them!"

"Oh no," said the boy casually. "I won't think much about them, mother. You needn't worry. I wouldn't worry, mother, if I were you."

"If you were me and I were you," said his mother, "I wonder what we *should* do!"

"But you know you needn't worry, mother, don't you?" the boy repeated.

"I should be awfully glad to know it," she said wearily.

"Oh, well, *you can*, you know. I mean, you *ought* to know you needn't worry," he insisted.

"Ought I? Then I'll see about it," she said.

Paul's secret of secrets was his wooden horse, that which had no name. Since he was emancipated from a nurse and a nursery-governess, he had had his rocking-horse removed to his own bedroom at the top of the house.

"Surely you're too big for a rocking-horse!" his mother had remonstrated.

"Well, you see, mother, till I can have a *real* horse, I like to have *some* sort of animal about," had been his quaint answer.

"Do you feel he keeps you company?" she laughed.

"Oh yes! He's very good, he always keeps me company, when I'm there," said Paul.

So the horse, rather shabby, stood in an arrested prance in the boy's bedroom.

The Derby was drawing near, and the boy grew more and more tense. He hardly heard what was spoken to him, he was very frail, and his eyes were really uncanny. His mother had sudden strange seizures

of uneasiness about him. Sometimes, for half an hour, she would feel
a sudden anxiety about him that was almost anguish. She wanted to
rush to him at once, and know he was safe.

Two nights before the Derby, she was at a big party in town, when
one of her rushes of anxiety about her boy, her first-born, gripped her
heart till she could hardly speak. She fought with the feeling, might
and main, for she believed in common sense. But it was too strong.
She had to leave the dance and go downstairs to telephone to the
country. The children's nursery-governess was terribly surprised and
startled at being rung up in the night.

"Are the children all right, Miss Wilmot?"

"Oh yes, they are quite all right."

"Master Paul? Is he all right?"

"He went to bed as right as a trivet. Shall I run up and look at
him?"

"No," said Paul's mother reluctantly. "No! Don't trouble. It's all
right. Don't sit up. We shall be home fairly soon." She did not want
her son's privacy intruded upon.

"Very good," said the governess.

It was about one o'clock when Paul's mother and father drove up to
their house. All was still. Paul's mother went to her room and slipped
off her white fur cloak. She had told her maid not to wait up for her.
She heard her husband downstairs, mixing a whiskey and soda.

And then, because of the strange anxiety at her heart, she stole
upstairs to her son's room. Noiselessly she went along the upper corridor. Was there a faint noise? What was it?

She stood, with arrested muscles, outside his door, listening. There
was a strange, heavy, and yet not loud noise. Her heart stood still. It
was a soundless noise, yet rushing and powerful. Something huge, in
violent, hushed motion. What was it? What in God's name was it?
She ought to know. She felt that she knew the noise. She knew what
it was.

Yet she could not place it. She couldn't say what it was. And on
and on it went, like a madness.

Softly, frozen with anxiety and fear, she turned the doorhandle.

The room was dark. Yet in the space near the window, she heard
and saw something plunging to and fro. She gazed in fear and amaze-
ment.

Then suddenly she switched on the light, and saw her son, in his
green pyjamas, madly surging on the rocking-horse. The blaze of light
suddenly lit him up, as he urged the wooden horse, and lit her up,
as she stood, blonde, in her dress of pale green and crystal, in the
doorway.

"Paul!" she cried. "Whatever are you doing?"

"It's Malabar!" he screamed in a powerful, strange voice. "It's Malabar!"

His eyes blazed at her for one strange and senseless second, as he ceased urging his wooden horse. Then he fell with a crash to the ground, and she, all her tormented motherhood flooding upon her, rushed to gather him up.

But he was unconscious, and unconscious he remained, with some brain-fever. He talked and tossed, and his mother sat stonily by his side.

"Malabar! It's Malabar! Bassett, Bassett, I *know!* It's Malabar!"

So the child cried, trying to get up and urge the rocking-horse that gave him his inspiration.

"What does he mean by Malabar?" asked the heart-frozen mother.

"I don't know," said the father stonily.

"What does he mean by Malabar?" she asked her brother Oscar.

"It's one of the horses running for the Derby," was the answer.

And, in spite of himself, Oscar Cresswell spoke to Bassett, and himself put a thousand on Malabar: at fourteen to one.

The third day of the illness was critical: they were waiting for a change. The boy, with his rather long, curly hair, was tossing ceaselessly on the pillow. He neither slept nor regained consciousness, and his eyes were like blue stones. His mother sat, feeling her heart had gone, turned actually into a stone.

In the evening, Oscar Cresswell did not come, but Bassett sent a message, saying could he come up for one moment, just one moment? Paul's mother was very angry at the intrusion, but on second thoughts she agreed. The boy was the same. Perhaps Bassett might bring him to consciousness.

The gardener, a shortish fellow with a little brown moustache and sharp little brown eyes, tiptoed into the room, touched his imaginary cap to Paul's mother, and stole to the bedside, staring with glittering, smallish eyes at the tossing, dying child.

"Master Paul!" he whispered. "Master Paul! Malabar came in first all right, a clean win. I did as you told me. You've made over seventy thousand pounds, you have; you've got over eighty thousand. Malabar came in all right. Master Paul."

"Malabar! Malabar! Did I say Malabar, mother? Did I say Malabar? Do you think I'm lucky, mother? I knew Malabar, didn't I? Over eighty thousand pounds! I call that lucky, don't you, mother? Over eighty thousand pounds! I knew, didn't I know I knew? Malabar came in all right. If I ride my horse till I'm sure, then I tell you, Bassett, you can go as high as you like. Did you go for all you were worth, Bassett?"

"I went a thousand on it, Master Paul."

"I never told you, mother, that if I can ride my horse, and *get there*, then I'm absolutely sure—oh, absolutely! Mother, did I ever tell you? I *am* lucky!"

"No, you never did," said his mother.

But the boy died in the night.

And even as he lay dead, his mother heard her brother's voice saying to her: "My God, Hester, you're eighty-odd thousand to the good, and a poor devil of a son to the bad. But, poor devil, poor devil, he's best gone out of a life where he rides his rocking-horse to find a winner."

Harry T. Moore

Some Notes on "The Rocking-Horse Winner"*

"The Rocking-Horse Winner" is a horrible commentary on today's money-madness—horrible because its evil forces crush the child in the story.

"The Rocking-Horse Winner" has some unusual elements: it is surprising to find in a Lawrence story even a partial knowledge of horse-racing and of the sporting world. It is one of the phases of life Lawrence usually ignored. Now and then there is mention of a "sporting" uncle, as in the autobiographical sketch "Rex" or the story "The Primrose Path," but there are no details of betting procedures or other related matters, as there are in "The Rocking-Horse Winner." And throughout Lawrence there is virtually no recognition of the football and cricket and boxing activities that take up so much of the time of modern man. There is, however, the description of the bullfight in *The Plumed Serpent,* and in the story "None of That" a bullfighter is one of the leading characters. But this is a different world from that of baseball or tennis or Rugby, or even of horse-racing: death is courted in the bull ring. Ernest Hemingway, who attended bullfights in order to improve his writing technique by learning how to describe action in the face of violent death, and violent death itself, says in *Death in the Afternoon* that "the bullfight is not a sport in the Anglo-Saxon sense of the word. . . . Rather it is a tragedy"—the dramatization of the conflict between man and beast. Lawrence did not become interested, as Hemingway did, in the mechanics of bullfighting: he used it as a social commentary on the observers, both Mexican and American, in *The Plumed Serpent,* and in "None of That" he

*Reprinted from *The Life and Works of D. H. Lawrence* (New York: Twayne Publishers, 1951), pp. 277-279, by permission. Title supplied by the editor.

described only Cuesta's extra-bull ring activities. And although he did not know the bullfighters' world intimately, he made Cuesta a believable character, suggesting by a few deft strokes the cruelty and viciousness of the man chilled into arrogance by years of adulation and the successful mastery of danger. "The Rocking-Horse Winner" presents a quite different picture of another corner of another kind of sporting world. /278/

It is, among other things, a story of the supernatural. As mentioned before, it was first printed in Lady Cynthia Asquith's *The Ghost Book: Sixteen New Stories of the Uncanny*. "The Rocking-Horse Winner" was certainly more appropriate for this collection than the presumed portrait of the Asquiths in "Glad Ghosts," which Lawrence had first considered submitting. "The Rocking-Horse Winner" is hardly a ghost story, however; Lady Cynthia's subtitle to her anthology has the proper label for Lawrence's contribution—a story of the uncanny. The satiric element occurs in connection with the family that is always grasping for money and always living beyond its means: the mother with her expensive tastes and the father who is described, with apposite vagueness, as going "in to town to some office." The mother does not love her children, but makes such a show of loving them that people say she adores them. The family's house is haunted by an unspoken phrase, "There must be more money!" The children hear it continually, though it is never spoken aloud; they hear it particularly at Christmas time as they play among their expensive toys.

The little boy, Paul—the only instance outside *Sons and Lovers* when Lawrence gives this name to a leading character—asks his mother why the family has no money, and she tells him it is because they have no luck. He says he is lucky, that God has told him so— and then he begins his uncanny rides on the toy horse that magically conveys to him the names of the winning race horses.

With the help of the gardener and of a sports-minded uncle, Paul without his parents' knowing it makes them increasingly richer. The story fills with the names of the great races and of the winning horses, providing a lurid and frantic background. And in the foreground there is the boy fiercely riding his rocking-horse, cajoling it, tearing his nerves apart, in the wild journey that can end only in death.

Lawrence has here written a study not only of the gambling neurosis—even the winners are destroyed—but also of the entire money neurosis that destroys so many modern families, often crushing the children. "The Rocking-Horse Winner," with its /279/ contagious excitement and its air of inescapable doom, is an important contribution to the literature of the uncanny. It is, in the truest sense, a horror

story. A successful film was made from it in England in 1949, starring
John Mills and Valerie Hobson, with John Howard Davis as Paul.
The scenarist and director, Anthony Pellissier, was uncustomarily
faithful to the original story.

W. D. Snodgrass

A Rocking-Horse: The Symbol, the Pattern, the Way to Live

> "Daddy! Daddy!" he cried to his father. "Daddy, look what they
> are doing! Daddy, they're beating the poor little horse!"
> —*Crime and Punishment*

"The Rocking-Horse Winner" seems the perfect story by the least
meticulous of serious writers. It has been anthologized, analyzed by
New Critics and force-fed to innumerable undergraduates. J. Arthur
Rank has filmed it. Yet no one has seriously investigated the story's
chief structural feature, the symbolic extensions of the rocking-horse
itself, and I feel that in ignoring several meaning-areas of this story
we ignore some of Lawrence's most stimulating thought.

Though the reach of the symbol is overwhelming, in some sense
the story is "about" its literal, narrative level: the life of the family
that chooses money instead of some more stable value, that takes
money as its nexus of affection. The first fault apparently lay with
the mother. The story opens:

> There was a woman who was beautiful, who started with all the
> advantages, yet she had no luck. She married for love, and the
> love turned to dust. She had bonny children, yet she felt they had
> been thrust upon her, and she could not love them . . . at the
> center of her heart was a hard little place that could not feel love,
> not for anybody.

*Reprinted from *The Hudson Review*, XI, No. 2 (Summer 1958), 191-200. Copyright © 1958 by The Hudson Review, Inc. Reprinted by permission of the author
and the journal.

We never learn much more about her problems, about *why* her love turned to dust. But the rhyming verb *thrust* is shrewdly chosen and placed; knowing Lawrence, we may well guess that Hester's dissatisfaction is, at least in large part, sexual. We needn't say that the sexual factor is the sole or even primary cause of her frigidity, but it is usually a major expression and index of it, and becomes causal. Lawrence wrote in an amazing letter to John Middleton Murry:

> A woman unsatisfied must have luxuries. But a woman who loves a man would sleep on a board. . . . You've tried to satisfy Katherine with what you could earn for her, give her: and she will only be satisfied with what you *are*. /192/

There could scarcely be a more apt description of Hester's situation. As for her husband, we cannot even guess what he *is*; he gives too few clues. Failing to supply the luxuries that both he and his wife demand, he has withdrawn, ceased to exist. The one thing he could always give —himself, the person he is—seems part of a discarded currency. The mother, the father, finally the boy—each in turn has withdrawn his vital emotions and affections from commitment in and to the family. Withdrawing, they have denied their own needs, the one thing that could be "known" and "sure." They have, instead, committed their lives to an external, money, and so to "luck," since all externals are finally beyond control and cannot be really known. Thus, it is Paul's attempt to bring an external into his control by knowledge which destroys him. It is a failure of definition.

The father's withdrawal, of course, leaves a gap which encourages Paul in a natural Oedipal urge to replace him. And money becomes the medium of that replacement. So the money in the story must be taken literally, but is also a symbolic substitute for love and affection (since it has that meaning to the characters themselves), and ultimately for sperm. We know that money is not, to Paul, a good in itself —it is only a way to win his mother's affection, "compel her attention," show her that *he* is lucky though his father is not. That money has no real use for Hester either becomes only too clear in that crucial scene where Paul sends her the birthday present of five thousand pounds hoping to alleviate her problems, relax the household, and so release her affections. His present only makes her colder, harder, more luxurious, and:

> . . . the voices in the house, behind the sprays of mimosa and almond blossom, and from under the piles of iridescent cushions,

simply trilled and screamed in a sort of ecstasy: "There *must* be more money! Oh-h-h; there *must* be more money. Oh, now, now-w! Now-w-w—there must be more money;—more than ever!"

The mother and father have driven themselves to provide the mother with what she, actually, needs least. And she has squandered it, one would guess, precisely to show her scorn for it and for the husband who provides it. Money as a symbolic substitute has only sharpened the craving it was meant to satisfy; the family has set up a vicious circle which will finally close upon Paul.

As several critics have noted, the story resembles many well-known fairy tales or magical stories in which the hero bargains with evil powers for personal advantages or forbidden knowledge. These /193/ bargains are always "rigged" so that the hero, after his apparent triumphs, will lose in the end—this being, in itself, the standard "moral." Gordon and Tate sum up their interpretation: "the boy, Paul, has invoked strange gods and pays the penalty with his death." Robert Gorham Davis goes on to point out that many witches supposedly rode hobby-horses of one sort or another (e.g., the witch's broom) to rock themselves into a magical and prophetic trance. When he rides, Paul's eyes glare blue and strange, he will speak to no one, his sisters fear him. He stares into the horse's wooden face: "Its red mouth was slightly open, its big eye was wide and glassy-bright." More and more engrossed in his doom as the story progresses, he becomes "wild-eyed and strange . . . his big blue eyes blazing with a sort of madness." We hear again and again of the uncanny blaze of his eyes until finally, at his collapse, they are "like blue stones." Clearly enough, he is held in some self-induced prophetic frenzy, a line of meaning carefully developed by the story. When Paul first asserts to his mother that he is "lucky," he claims that God told him so. This seems pure invention, yet may well be a kind of *hubris,* considering the conversation that had just passed with his mother:

"Nobody ever knows why one person is lucky and another unlucky."
"Don't they? Nobody at all? Does nobody know?"
"Perhaps God. But He never tells."

Whether Paul really believes that God told him so, he certainly does become lucky. And others come to believe that superhuman powers are involved. Bassett thinks of "Master Paul" as a seer and takes an explicitly worshipful tone towards him. He grows "serious as a church" and twice tells Uncle Oscar in a "secret, religious voice. . . . 'It's as if he had it from heaven.' " These hints of occultism culminate in Uncle Oscar's benediction:

> "My God, Hester, you're eighty-odd thousand to the good, and a poor devil of a son to the bad. But poor devil, poor devil, he's best gone out of a life where he rides his rocking-horse to find a winner."

So, in some sense, Paul *is* demonic, yet a poor devil; though he has compacted with evil, his intentions were good and he has destroyed only himself. At first metaphorically, in the end literally, he has committed suicide. But that may be, finally, the essence of evil.

It is clear, then, that the story is talking about some sort of /194/ religious perversion. But *what* sort? Who are the strange gods: how does Paul serve them and receive their information? We must return here, I think, to the problem of knowledge and intellection. Paul is destroyed, we have said, by his desire to "know." It is not only that he has chosen wrong ways of knowing or wrong things to know. The evil is that he *has* chosen to know, to live by intellection. Lawrence wrote, in a letter to Ernest Collings:

> My great religion is a belief in the blood, the flesh, as being wiser than the intellect. We can go wrong in our minds. But what our blood feels and believes and says, is always true. *The intellect is only a bit and bridle.* What do I care about knowledge. . . . I conceive a man's body as a kind of flame . . . and the intellect is just the light that is shed on to the things around. . . . A flame isn't a flame because it lights up two, or twenty objects on a table. It's a flame because it is itself. And we have forgotten ourselves. . . . The real way of living is to answer to one's wants. Not "I want to light up with my intelligence as many things as possible" but ". . . I want that liberty, I want that woman, I want that pound of peaches, I want to go to sleep, I want to go to the pub and have a good time, I want to look a beastly swell today, I want to kiss that girl, I want to insult that man."

(I have italicized the bit and bridle metaphor to underscore an immediate relationship to the rocking-horse of the story.)

Not one member of this family really knows his wants. Like most idealists, they have ignored the most important part of the command *Know thyself*, and so cannot deal with their most important problem, their own needs. To know one's needs is really to know one's own limits, hence one's definition. Lawrence's notion of living by "feeling" or "blood" (as opposed to "knowledge," "mind" or "personality") may be most easily understood, perhaps, as living according to what you *are*, not what you think you should be made over into; knowing yourself, not external standards. Thus, what Lawrence calls "feeling" could well be glossed as "knowing one's wants." Paul's family, lacking true knowledge of themselves, have turned their light, their intellect, outward, hoping to control the external world. The mother, refusing to clarify what her emotions really *are*, hopes to control herself and her world by acting "gentle and anxious for her children." She tries to be or act what she thinks she should be, not taking adequate notice of what she is and needs. She acts from precepts about motherhood, not from recognition of her own will, self-respect for her own motherhood. Thus, the apparent contradiction between Hester's coldness, the "hard . . . /195/ center of her heart," and, on the other hand, "all her tormented motherhood flooding upon her" when Paul collapses near the end of the story. Some deep source of affection has apparently lain hidden (and so tormented) in her, all along; it was her business to find and release it sooner. Similarly, Paul has a need for affection which he does not, and perhaps cannot, understand or manage: Like his mother, he is trying to cover this lack of self-knowledge with knowledge about the external world, which he hopes will bring him a fortune, and so affection.

Paul is, so, a symbol of civilized man, whipping himself on in a nervous endless "mechanical gallop," an "arrested prance," in chase of something which will destroy him if he ever catches it, and which he never really wanted anyway. He is the scientist, teacher, theorist, who must always know about the outside world so that he can manipulate it to what he believes is his advantage. Paradoxically, such knowledge comes to him only in isolation, in withdrawal from the physical world, so that his intellect may operate upon it unimpeded. And such control of the world as he can gain is useless because he has lost the knowledge of what he wants, what he is.

This, then, is another aspect of the general problem treated by the story. A still more specific form of withdrawal and domination is suggested by the names of the horses on which Paul bets. Those names—like the names of the characters—are a terrible temptation to ingenuity. One should certainly be wary of them. Yet two of them seem related to each other and strongly suggest another area into which the story's basic pattern extends. Paul's first winner, Singhalese, and his last, Malabar, have names which refer to British colonial regions of India. (A third name, Mirza, suggests "Mirzapur"—still another colonial region. But that is surely stretching things.) India is obviously one of the focal points of the modern disease of colonial empire; for years Malabar and Singhalese were winners for British stockholders and for the British people in general. The British, like any colonial power or large government or corporation, have gambled upon and tried to control peoples and materials which they never see and with which they never have any vital physical contacts. (Lawrence's essay "Men must Work and Women as Well" is significant here.) They have lived by the work of others, one of the chief evils of which is that their own physical energies have no outlet and are turned into dissatisfactions /196/ and pseudo-needs which must be filled with more and more luxuries. And so long as they "knew," placed their bets right, they were rich, were able to afford more and more dissatisfactions. A similar process destroyed Spain: a similar process destroyed Paul.

Though these last several areas of discussion are only tenuously present, most readers would agree, I think, that the rocking-horse reaches symbolically toward such meanings: into family economy and relations, into the occult, into the modern intellectual spirit, into the financial and imperial manipulations of the modern State. But surely the sexual area is more basic to the story—is, indeed, the basic area in which begins the pattern of living which the rocking-horse symbolizes. It is precisely this area of the story and its interpretation which has been ignored, perhaps intentionally, by other commentators. Oddly enough, Lawrence himself has left an almost complete gloss of this aspect of the story in his amazing, infuriating, and brilliant article, "Pornography and Obscenity." There, Lawrence defines pornography not as art which stimulates sexual desire, but rather as art which contrives to make sex ugly (if only by excluding it) and so leads the observer away from sexual intercourse and toward masturbation. He continues:

> When the grey ones wail that the young man and young woman went and had sexual intercourse, they are bewailing the fact that the young man and the young woman didn't go separately and masturbate. Sex must go somewhere, especially in young people. So, in our glorious civilization, it goes in masturbation. And the mass of our popular literature, the bulk of our popular amusements just exists to provoke masturbation. . . . The moral guardians who are prepared to censor all open and plain portrayal of sex must now be made to give their only justification: We prefer that the people shall masturbate.

Even a brief reading of the essay should convince one that Paul's mysterious ecstasy is not only religious, but sexual and onanistic. That is Paul's "secret of secrets." Just as the riding of a horse is an obvious symbol for the sex act, and "riding" was once the common sexual verb, so the rocking-horse stands for the child's imitation of the sex act, for the riding which goes nowhere.

We note in the passage quoted above that Lawrence thinks of masturbation chiefly as a substitute for some sort of intercourse. Similarly in the story:

> "Surely, you're too big for a rocking-horse!" his mother had remonstrated. /197/
>
> "Well, you see, mother, till I can have a *real* horse, I like to have some sort of animal about," had been his quaint answer.

This is one of several doctrinal points where the reader will likely disagree with Lawrence. Nonetheless, the idea was prevalent at the time of writing and is common enough today that most men probably still think of masturbation chiefly as a sex substitute. And like the money substitute mentioned before, it can only famish the craving it is thought to ease. So we find another area in which the characters of the story don't know what they need; another and narrower vicious circle.

The tightening of that circle, the destruction of Paul, is carefully defined; here, one feels both agreement with Lawrence's thought and a strong admiration for his delineation of the process:

> . . . He went off by himself, vaguely, in a childish way, seeking for the clue to "luck." Absorbed, taking no heed of other people, he went about with a sort of stealth, seeking inwardly for luck.

Stealth becomes more and more a part of Paul. We hear again and again of his secret, his "secret within a secret," we hear his talk with Uncle Oscar:

> "I shouldn't like mother to know I was lucky," said the boy.
>
> "Why not, son?"
>
> "She'd stop me."
>
> "I don't think she would."
>
> "Oh!"—and the boy writhed in an odd way—"I *don't* want her to know, uncle."

We may quote here a passage from "Pornography and Obscenity":

> Masturbation is the one thoroughly secret act of the human being, more secret even than excrementation.

Naturally, any act accompanied by such stealth is damaging to the personality and to its view of itself. It involves an explicit denial of the self, a refusal to affirm the self and its acts (an imaginative suicide) and consequently a partial divorce from reality. But this is only part of that same general process of isolation. In the essay, Lawrence says:

> Most of the responses are dead, most of the awareness is dead, nearly all the constructive activity is dead, and all that remains is a sort of a shell, a half empty creature fatally self-preoccupied and incapable of either giving or taking. . . . And this is masturbation's result. Enclosed within /198/ the vicious circle of the self, with no vital contacts outside, the self becomes emptier and emptier, till it is almost a nullus, a nothingness.

And this is the process dramatized by the story. Paul drawn back from his family, bit by bit, until he becomes strange and fearful to his sisters and will speak to no one, has grown beyond the nurse and has no real contact with his parents. Even Uncle Oscar feels uncomfortable around him. Finally he has moved his rocking-horse away from the family and taken it with him "to his own bedroom at the top of the house."

Lawrence believes that man's isolation is an unavoidable part of his definition as a human being—yet he needs all the contact he can possibly find. In his essay on Poe, Lawrence writes:

> Love is the mysterious vital attraction which draws things together, closer, closer together. For this reason sex is the actual crisis of love. For in sex the two blood-systems, in the male and female, concentrate and come into contact, the merest film intervening. Yet if the intervening film breaks down, it is death. . . .
>
> In sensual love, it is the two blood-systems, the man's and the woman's, which sweep up into pure contact, and almost *fuse*. Almost mingle. Never quite. There is always the finest imaginable wall between the two blood waves, through which pass unknown vibrations, forces, but through which the blood itself must never break, or it means bleeding.

Sex, then, is man's closest link to other human beings and to the "unknown," his surest link into humanity, and it is this that Paul and his family have foresworn in their wilful isolation. And this isolation is more than physical. Again in "Pornography and Obscenity," we find:

The great danger of masturbation lies in its merely exhaustive nature. In sexual intercourse, there is a give and take. A new stimulus enters as the native stimulus departs. Something quite new is added as the old surcharge is removed. And this is so in all sexual intercourse where two creatures are concerned, even in the homosexual intercourse. But in masturbation there is nothing but loss. There is no reciprocity. There is merely the spending away of a certain force, and no return. The body remains, in a sense, a corpse, after the act of self-abuse.

To what extent Lawrence thinks this reciprocity, this give and take, to be physical, I am not sure; I *am* sure it could easily be exaggerated. Lawrence makes a sharp distinction between the physical and the material. At any rate, it seems to me that the most /199/ important aspect of this sexual give-and-take is certainly emotional and psychological and that the stimulus which enters in sexual intercourse lies in coming to terms with an actual sexual partner who is real and in no wise "ideal." Thus, such a partner will afford both unexpectable pleasures and very real difficulties which must be recognized and overcome. But in masturbation these problems can be avoided. Most psychologists would agree that the most damaging thing about masturbation is that it is almost always accompanied by fantasy about intercourse with some "ideal" partner. Thus, one is led away from reality with its difficulties and unpredictable joys, into the self and its repetitive fantasies. This may seem rather far from the story, but I suggest that this explains the namelessness of the rocking-horse. (It also, of course, suggests shame and is valuable in manipulating the plot.) The real partner has a name which is always the same and stands for a certain configuration of personality with its quirks and glories; the fantasy partner, having no personality, has no name of his or her own but is given the name of such "real" partners as one might wish from week to week.

These, then, are the gods which Paul has invoked. This sexual problem gives, also, a startling range of irony to the religious texture of the story. The "secret within a secret . . . that which had no name" comes to be not only the shame of Paul's masturbation, but also a vicious and astounding parody of the "word within a word" — that which cannot be named. It should be clear from the material already quoted, and even more so from a reading of "Pornography and Obscenity," that it is popular religion — Christian idealism — that Lawrence is attacking, for it supports the "purity lie" and leaves masturbation as the only sexual expression, even at times openly condoning it. The strange gods are the familiar ones; the occult heresy is popular Christian piety.

It is not clear, however, how Paul receives knowledge from his onanistic gods. Lawrence himself does not pretend to know *how* this comes about, he only knows that it does exist:

> The only positive effect of masturbation is that it seems to release a certain mental energy, in some people. But it is mental energy which manifests itself always in the same way, in a vicious circle of analysis and impotent criticism, or else a vicious circle of false and easy sympathy, sentimentalities. This sentimentalism and the niggling analysis, often self-analysis, of most of our modern literature, is a sign of self-abuse. /200/

This momentary release of energy is, I take it, equivalent to finding the name of the "winner" in the story. Thus the two great meaning-streams of the story, intellection and masturbation, relate. Masturbation stands as the primary area: the withdrawal and stealth, the intellectual participation in the physical, the need to know and magically control the external, the driving of the self into a rigid, "mechanical gallop," the displacement of motive, the whole rejection of self, all begins here. And the pattern, once established, spreads, gradually infecting all the areas of life, familial, economic, political, religious. Here, again, the reader may feel a doctrinal disagreement, suspecting that masturbation is more symptomatic than causal. Such disagreement scarcely touches the story, however, whose business is not to diagnose or cure, but to create a vision of life, which it does with both scope and courage.

I want to quote finally, one more passage from the essay "Pornography and Obscenity" to round off the argument and tie up some loose ends, and also simply because of its value, its sincerity. It is a kind of summation of the story's meaning and opens with a sentence roughly equivalent to Uncle Oscar's judgment: "he's best gone out of a life where he rides a rocking-horse to find a winner":

> If my life is merely to go on in a vicious circle of self-enclosure, masturbating self-consciousness, it is worth nothing to me. If my individual life is to be enclosed within the huge corrupt lie of society today, purity and the dirty little secret, then it is worth not much to me. Freedom is a very great reality. But it means, above all things, freedom from lies. It is, first, freedom from myself; from the lie of my all-importance, even to myself; it is

freedom from the self-conscious masturbating thing I am, self-enclosed. And second, freedom from the vast lie of the social world, the lie of purity and the dirty little secret. All the other monstrous lies lurk under the cloak of this one primary lie. The monstrous lie of money lurks under the cloak of purity. Kill the purity-lie and the money-lie will be defenseless.

We have to be sufficiently conscious, and self-conscious, to know our own limits and to be aware of the greater urge within us and beyond us. Then we cease to be primarily interested in ourselves. Then we learn to leave ourselves alone, in all the affective centres: not to force our feelings in any way, and never to force our sex. Then we make the great onslaught on the outside lie, the inside lie being settled. And that is freedom and the fight for freedom.

There are few more courageous statements in our literature.

Carolyn Gordon and Allen Tate

Commentary on "The Rocking-Horse Winner"*

"The Rocking-Horse Winner" is the story of a boy who came by his death in an effort to escape a situation which he finds intolerable. The point of view is that of the Concealed Narrator. There are a few panoramas, skilfully timed, but for the most part the story consists of "blocks" of action which seem to have the solidity and dimensions of life itself. There are one or two passages in which Lawrence sacrifices this objectivity and tells you what is going on in his young hero's mind instead of rendering it in terms of action, but these passages do not occur at crucial moments, as in "The Princess," for instance, and do not seem to weaken the pattern appreciably. /228/

The Complication is the situation of the hero, a little boy named Paul, who is unusually sensitive. For him the house he lives in is haunted; voices continually whisper: "There must be more money!" When he asks his mother why they haven't any more money she replies that it is because they are unlucky. Lawrence prepares for the Resolution (see p. 11) when Paul defies the supernatural voices, declaring stoutly, "Well, anyhow, I'm lucky."

In the Resolution Paul discovers, through association with a sporting gardener, that if he rides his rocking horse long enough and madly enough he "knows" the name of the winner of whatever horse race he and the gardener are interested in. The gardener places his bets for him. Paul amasses a little fortune and puts it at his mother's disposal, but the voices whisper more shrilly than ever. He places a few bets when he is not "sure" and goes down, determined to retrieve his fortunes with the Grand National and the Lincoln, but they both go

*Reprinted from *The House of Fiction* (2nd ed.; New York: Charles Scribner's Sons, 1960), pp. 227-230, by permission.

by and he is not "sure." He is all the more determined to "know" for
the Derby and, riding his rocking-horse harder than ever, rides across
the boundary of the visible world and, screaming the name of the
winner, collapses and dies.

It should be observed how one block of action springs out of the
preceding block. When Uncle Oscar sees Paul riding his rocking horse
he asks the horse's name. But the boy tells him he has "different
names. He was called Sansovino last week."

"Sansovino, eh? Won the Ascot. How did you know his name?"

"He always talks horse races with Bassett," Paul's elder sister, Joan,
says. She has previously remarked to the nurse: "He's always riding
like that. I wish he'd leave off." Thus, in an apparently casual inter-
change between a little girl and her nurse and an uncle and his
nephew, important parts of the story's Complication are provided for.
The uncle's man-of-the-world curiosity about his small nephew's interest in racing (the mechanism by which the action is made to un-
wind) is established and Joan's reference to Bassett prepares us for
the partnership between Paul and the gardener, while her remark to
the nurse indicates that Paul's behavior seems strange and even repel-
lent to a normal child.

The Enveloping Action is represented by the mother. It is her attitude towards life that fills the house with the whispers that start the
boy on his race towards death. The envelopment not only furnishes
the background but has its own dramatic action. At a key moment,
midway of the story, the direct presentation is suspended and a
panoramic view, belonging to the Enveloping Action, flows in and
tightens the main current of the story so that it hurls itself faster
towards its goal. This panorama—the occasion on which the boy puts
five thousand pounds at his mother's disposal—is presented in brilliant detail, muted only by "distance." And yet the voices in the
house, behind the sprays of mimosa and almond blossom, and from
the piles of iridescent cushions, trilled and screamed in a kind of
ecstasy: "There *must* be more money! . . . Now-w-w there *must* be
more money!" /229/

Again, action which sets forth the enveloping life of Paul's mother,
comes to the front on an evening two nights before the Derby, when
she has one of her "rushes of anxiety" about the boy and she and his
father come home early from a party, and the mother, stealing along
the corridor to the boy's room, hears a "strange, heavy, and yet not
loud noise. . . . Something huge, in violent, hushed motion," and opening the door, sees and hears something plunging in the space near the
window.

The Enveloping Action — that is, the social *milieu* — also has the last word dramatically. As the boy lies dead his mother hears Uncle Oscar, who, "in spite of himself put a thousand on Malabar at fourteen to one," say to her: "My God, Hester, you're eighty-odd thousand to the good, and a poor devil of a son to the bad. But, poor devil, poor devil, he's best gone out of a life where he rides his rocking-horse to find a winner."

The details are beautifully rendered throughout the story. The pivot on which the action turns, the fact that the family does not have as much money as the mother thinks it should have, is presented with dramatic objectivity:

"Mother," said the boy Paul one day, "why don't we keep a car of our own? Why do we always use uncle's, or else a taxi?"

Uncle Oscar — all we need to know about him is that he was handsome, had a fine car, a heart in his bosom and tongue in his head — speaks always admirably in character:

"Say, Paul, old man, do you ever put anything on a horse?" And when the boy, watching him closely, parries with, "Why, do you think I oughtn't to?" he replies with easy camaraderie, "Not a bit of it! I thought perhaps you might give me a tip for the Lincoln."

This remark arouses our admiration by its verisimilitude. It is exactly the kind of thing an amiable, sympathetic uncle might say to a small boy, but it also introduces an important part of the action: the fact that Paul cannot give his uncle a tip on the Lincoln contributes to his death. These solid, dimensional effects contribute a great deal to the dramatic impact of the story.

Many of the details have a double signficance, playing their roles in the action, even while they point it up. We see Paul descending from his first gallop and standing with "his blue eyes still flaring, and his sturdy long legs straddling apart." At the same time, the fact that his blue eyes are set rather close together prepares us for his fanatical pursuit of luck. Bassett, the gardener, has the serious demeanor of the well-trained upper servant. Lawrence's repeated use of the word "religious" in describing him prepares us by indirection for the revelation of the boy's being in the grip of a supernatural power.

At the climax of the story the mother opens her son's door and sees him "in his green pyjamas, madly surging on the rocking-horse." The blaze of light suddenly lit him up as he urged the wooden horse on and *lit her up* as she stood, blonde in her dress of pale green and crystal in the doorway.

Lawrence uses here—unconsciously, no doubt—a technique which is the solid underpinning of all Henry James's later work: the rendering of an object or person through reference to another object or person. We see the son through the eyes of the mother; we see the mother through the eyes of the son. The two viewpoints fuse to make a rounded whole.

Lawrence shows a rare objectivity in his use of symbolism/230/in this story. Again, he reminds us of James, seeming to be determined in this one instance, at least, to let his "message" present itself through symbolic action rather than through exhortation or preachment. The rocking horse is a link between the visible and invisible worlds and is his prime symbol. The horse behaves with traditional sibylline calm. When the boy stares appealingly into its face, its red mouth remains slightly open, its big eyes are wide and glassy-bright.

This story has extraordinary Tonal Unity. Carefully chosen cadences play their part in the dramatic effect. The first paragraph begins: "There was a woman who was beautiful, who started with all the advantages, yet she had no luck," an admirable preparation for what follows.

The whispering voices also play an important part in the tonal effect, as does Bassett's speech to the dying boy which has the urgent, almost nonsensical quality of any speech made by the living to the dying. The name of the winner, too, is important.

"It's Malabar!" he screamed, in a powerful, strange voice. "It's Malabar!"

Let the student substitute a name like "Little Andy" or "Sea Biscuit" for the winner and see what a difference such a substitution will make in the whole story. The combinations of short a's and broad a's has a tragic sound and the word "Malabar" itself strikes our ear strangely. (Joyce achieves the same effect with his title, "Araby.") To sum up: the boy, Paul, has invoked strange gods and pays the penalty with his death.

Robert Gorham Davis

Observations on "The Rocking-Horse Winner"*

This story begins like a fairy tale, and maintains an appropriately simple, rapidly flowing style throughout. Notice the short paragraphs, the short sentences, the repetitions and recurrences, the exclamations and questions. Most of the story is in dialogue, and here too the speeches are very brief, with the characters repeating each other's phrases, or answering each other's queries.

The thematic words are "luck" and "money." They are brought together by the boy's mistake about "lucker," the kind of portmanteau word we find in *Finnegan's Wake*. The boy has luck — or a magic power born of his desperate need — and it wins him money. But magic power, we know from the fairy tales, is dangerous. The granting of wishes is always attended by severe conditions, or what is wished for has to be paid for in unexpected ways. Here, as in the famous story, "The Monkey's Paw," which most of the students surely know, the price is the son's death.

Though the boy's power is a magic one, the story is thoroughly realistic in theme, construction, and circumstantial detail. At the heart of the matter is an incapacity for love. This is true also of "The Prussian Officer," though it is so different in other respects. Let the students see in how many stories in this collection there is inability to love or to express love. What, in each case, are the causes and consequences? Here the mother cannot love, and seeks satisfaction instead in social status, in material display, in spending for the sake of spending. In this she becomes a representative of all the restless, neurotic people in the Western world who are dominated by a need for money,

*Reprinted from *Instructor's Manual* for *Ten Modern Masters: An Anthology of the Short Story* (2nd Ed.; New York: Harcourt, Brace & World, Inc. 1959), pp. 49-50, by permission. Copyright 1953 © 1959, by Harcourt, Brace & World, Inc.

a need further stimulated by mass advertising, with its emphasis on having and consuming. The complication in the story occurs on page 18, beginning with the sentence "Then something very curious happened." It reveals the essential horror of this void which cannot be filled. There had been a problem, the need for money, which the boy had set out to solve. When he makes such a handsome gift to his mother, he naturally thinks he has solved it. But since this is not what she really needs as a human being, the gift simply increases the mother's neurotic, insatiable hunger. And so the boy goes desperately on. Along with this intensification, which creates mounting dramatic tension in the story, goes the pattern of successive revelation. There is a reference on page 19 to "a secret within a secret."

What is revealed is all made very plausible. The world of betting and horse races has been a frequent source of excitement in popular fiction. Lawrence never showed much interest in it, but there he seems well informed. The boy's participation is sufficiently explained by the fact that this is a gambling family, and that Bassett is such a "perfect blade" of the turf. The details of the wagers are as carefully worked out as the bargaining over the dog in "Shingles for the Lord." Students may compare a humorous treatment of similar divinatory powers in the play "Three Men on a Horse." The motion of a furiously ridden rocking horse /50/ makes a good symbol of feverish activity that leads nowhere. But the use of a horse has psychological and folklorist appropriateness, too. *Myth and Ritual in Dance, Game and Rhyme* (1947) by Lewis Spence, pages 167-70 and *passim*, has some fascinating material about the use of hobbyhorses in folk rituals and by witches and seers who rock themselves into a trance that gives them magic knowledge.

Kingsley Widmer

The Triumph of the
Middleclass Matriarch*

Let us examine some of the other fictions in which the middle-class
matriarch has triumphed. While these stories do not deal with the
state bureaucracy and the industrial machine — the larger order of
things that men appear to control — the fictions nonetheless concern
the basic social order. Not only do women maintain the mass sentiments that create human identification with the largest things, they
also translate the rule of things into the area of personal relations.
(Lawrence generally dramatizes his industrialists — Gerald in *Women
in Love* and Clifford in *Lady Chatterley's Lover* — as emasculated
men.) Thus the female psyche expresses the deepest currents of contemporary society for Lawrence. Three stories, all relatively late
fictions — *The Rocking-Horse Winner, The Lovely Lady,* and *Mother
and Daughter* — show the modern matriarch turning sons, love, and
self into things.

The Rocking-Horse Winner is one of Lawrence's best-known and
most praised stories. This neat piece utilizes, in a Balzacean sense, a
money plot and theme. In a letter written about the time of the writing of this story, Lawrence said: "Perhaps it's really true, lucky in
money, unlucky in love." This old adage, with its antithesis of love
and money, which so appealed to Lawrence, appears to be the literal
source of the sardonic fairy-tale theme:

> There was a woman who was beautiful, who started with all the
> advantages, yet she had no luck. She married for love, and the
> love turned to dust. She had bonny children, yet she felt they had

*Reprinted from *The Art of Perversity*. (Seattle: University of Washington Press,
1962), pp. 92-95, by permission. Title supplied by the editor.

been thrust upon her, and she could not love them. . . . She herself knew that at the centre of her heart was a hard little place that could not feel love, no, not for anybody. Everybody else said of her: "She is such a good mother. /93/ She adores her children." Only she herself, and her children themselves, knew it was not so. They read it in each other's eyes.

They were a boy and two little girls. They lived in a pleasant house, with a garden, and they had discreet servants, and felt themselves superior to anyone in the neighbourhood.

Although they lived in style, they felt always an anxiety in the house. There was never enough money.

The mockingly simple exposition, with its devices from the children's story of the beautiful lady with the hard heart and the doubled pronouns for clarity, schematically pictures an upper-middle-class family attempting to keep up appearances and expensive tastes. The mother explains her version of magic to her son: "If you're lucky you have money. That's why it's better to be born lucky than rich. If you're rich you may lose your money. But if you're lucky, you will always get more money." Using another fairy-tale technique, Lawrence dramatizes the inner consciousness of his characters by projecting their feelings into inanimate objects. Thus, the stylish house itself whispers: *"There must be more money! There must be more money!"*

Appropriately to the form, the hero is a child, Paul, with "uncanny cold fire" and heightened sensitivity. Paul, the not-truly-loved child of an avaricious mother, may be a parabolic version of the autobiographical Paul of *Sons and Lovers.* In both fictions the exceptional son wishes to stop the whisperings of anxiety and prove himself to his mother. He forlornly hopes that by some magic of money success he can obtain love, but false magic leads only to death.

The child, "absorbed, taking no heed of other people . . . went about with a sort of stealth, seeking inwardly for luck." The "secret of secrets" resides in his rocking horse. Though past the age of such a toy, the boy insists on having it in his room at the top of the house (the fairy-tale magic tower?) and justifies it to his mother with the "quaint answer" that he wants the rocking horse until he can have "a *real* horse" because he likes "to have *some* sort of animal about." For Lawrence, we recall, /94/ horses symbolize the passions. The rocking horse provides the masturbatory toy counterfeit of passion in the middle-class world, as the modern gambling race track provides the public counterfeit of the heroic riders of the past.

Paul "madly" rides back and forth on his rocking horse in a trancelike state until "sure" about what horse to bet on in the big races. The terrible inner strain of such magic does not always succeed, but when the boy "knows (*feels* certain) he bets heavily, with the help of the horse-playing gardener, and wins. The boy's Uncle Oscar, a "mildly cynical" horseplayer, and one of those people with money luck, shows the usual shrewdness of the lucky; he worms out Paul's secret and joins in on the betting. Uncle Oscar also arranges Paul's gift to his mother of five thousand pounds from his winnings. Paul hopes the money, disguised as an anonymous legacy, will bring love instead of the whisperings of anxiety to the house. But the money only makes the mother more "cold, determined," more extravagant, and greedy for yet more money. Instead of joy, the house goes "mad" with a crescendo of "there *must* be more money . . . more than ever!"

Paul rocks away for magical luck in the Derby, the biggest horse race of all. On the last night before the race, his mother, with a sudden illumination of maternal anguish at a party, rushes home to find her son frenziedly swaying on his rocking horse. Paul screams out the name of the Derby winner, and the gardener and uncle place the bets. But for the boy delirium ends the sexually mad race for money, briefly interrupted by the knowledge of winning seventy thousand pounds, and his last words: "Mother, did I ever tell you? I *am* lucky." He dies, lucky in money but not, in this paradigmatic bourgeois home, lucky in mothers or love.

The cruel irony of the conclusion comes in the money-lucky uncle's comment to the mother: "You're eighty-odd thousand to the good, and a poor devil of a son to the bad. But, poor devil, poor devil, he's best gone out of a life where he rides his rocking- /95/ horse to find a winner." And so he is — but how else do poor devils make money? Or even well-to-do ones, like the uncle who has made a tidy sum from Paul's magic which he so disdains? Good and decent people all — the bourgeois are decent and affectionate, Lawrence allows — and no one really believes in going *that* far to make money. However, as a matter of fact, the good and decent mothers and uncles do go that far to make money, both because it provides the only full passion of their lives and because only through such total commitment can money really be made.

The Rocking-Horse Winner, a "well made" fiction, "objectively" imparts most of its vital information dramatically by the boy's dialogues with his mother and uncle. The shrewd dialogue, the economical delineation of figures in a set milieu, the allegorical neatness of the whispering house and magical rocking horse, the lack of the usual Lawrencean editorial intrusions, and the precise irony of the luck not worth having, make this a superior story. However, such aesthetic neatness is also a limitation — Lawrence, after all, has turned his magical perception of reality to haunting a house and a hobby horse in order to turn a moral — and the admirable attributes of the "well made fiction" should not be used to denigrate other and quite different fictions of Lawrence's. The artistic detachment and precision of the Flaubertian and Jamesian traditions, and of *The Rocking-Horse Winner,* create one kind of fiction, but not the sole criterion for imaginative prose.

Two of the premises implicit in *The Rocking-Horse Winner* — the negative power of money and the poignancy of the mother and son relation — receive even harsher exploration in a longer story, *The Lovely Lady.* In both of these mother-son stories it appears that Lawrence, like many artists, played agonized variations on one of his nuclear personal experiences. Because of this, the stories implicitly ask the reader to accept the rather extreme convention of cannibalistic mothers.

Roy Lamson, Hallett Smith, Hugh Maclean,
Wallace W. Douglas

A Critical Analysis*

This story could be described, on one level, as a tale of a boy who
gave his life in a futile attempt to provide his insatiable mother with
enough money. Approached differently, it might be seen as a kind of
ghost story in which the main interest lies in the mystery of the un-
explained power which enabled the boy to pick the winner in a horse
race. Incomplete or distorted analyses of the story might pursue either
of these directions and neglect the other. A close examination of Lawrence's methods, however, will show how the two elements fit together
and how the story at once arouses and satisfies the reader's interest in
a melodramatic suspense, in "psychology," and in a theme.

The story begins very simply: "There was a woman who was beautiful, who started with all the advantages, yet she had no luck." It is
almost the style of a fairy tale, and the fresh, naive style is important
in putting the reader in the frame of mind necessary for the story
which is to follow. We must, in fact, believe something which has no
obvious natural explanation, so we are urged subtly to adopt for a
moment that kind of wonder and suspension of disbelief which we
used to feel when we read Grimm or Hans Christian Andersen. As
the story progresses, however, this style changes and becomes more
intense. It is directly related to the mounting excitement of the story,
with the psychological element in it.

How much is psychological and how much is moral? In the first
place, the reader must recognize that the attitude toward horse racing
and betting on the horses is thoroughly British; there is no hint in the

---

*Reprinted from *The Critical Reader* (Rev. Ed.; W. W. Norton & Company, Inc.,
1949, © 1962), pp. 542-547, by permission. Copyright 1949, © 1962 by W. W. Norton
& Company, Inc.

story of disapproval of betting *as such.* The moral concern is rather over the quality in some people which /543/ always makes them want more money. This moral concern is developed psychologically: the need for more money in the family is presented, not as something that anybody says, not as an external fact established in the story by a glance at the family bank book or the mention of a pile of bills on the first of the month, but as something *felt.*

> And so the house came to be haunted by the unspoken phrase:
> There must be more money! There must be more money!

This is the kind of haunted house which even the most skeptical reader will be prepared to accept, and Lawrence reinforces the effect by relating the whisper to the children's expensive toys:

> The children could hear it all the time, though nobody said it aloud. They heard it at Christmas, when the expensive and splendid toys filled the nursery. Behind the shining modern rocking-horse, behind the smart doll's house, a voice would start whispering. . . .

It is a short step from this point to attributing the feeling to the toys themselves: ". . . even the horse, bending his wooden, champing head, heard it." By this innocent and subtle method the reader is prepared for the tremendous role of the rocking-horse in the climax of the story. But even more important, the *antagonist* in the story has been created. Here is the force against which the hero is to throw himself and perish.

If such a disembodied force is to be a character in the story, there must be careful handling of the characters who are people, so that the composition does not become confused. Notice how vague are the outlines of Paul's mother and father. The father is described as going into town to "some office," and when the mother tries to earn money, she is said to try "this thing and the other." The mother is not even named—she is always Paul's mother—until the very end of the story, when she is no longer Paul's mother and the author allows Oscar to call her by her name, Hester.

The central role of Paul in the story demands careful atten- /544/ tion. Frequently Lawrence takes us close to the point of view of Paul, and some readers might say that the vagueness about his father's business or his mother's attempts to make money merely indicates the normal child's vagueness about such matters. But the story cannot really be told from Paul's point of view, for several reasons. The suspense of the story would be ruined if the reader knew immediately all that went on in Paul's mind. The "secret within a secret" could not be held back from the reader. Moreover, the emotional quality of the ending would be changed; if we had followed the story exclusively through Paul's eyes and feelings, the ending would be pathetic and maudlin. As it is, there is enough distance so that a tragic feeling is possible.

As mediators between the reader's natural skepticism and the fantasy element in the plot stand Uncle Oscar and Bassett. They are both men of practical common sense, Bassett with his repeated "It's as if he had it from heaven" and his respectful suggestion to his social superior that when you have a good thing you shouldn't refuse it just because you don't understand it—"If Master Paul offers you to be partners, sir, I would, if I were you; if you'll excuse me"—and Uncle Oscar with his sense of humor and his cautious indulgence of his nephew. Oscar is developed very fully. He is introduced first unobtrusively, as the owner of the car which Paul's family borrows, as the source of the phrase "filthy lucre" which confused Paul, as the donor of the whip, the unconscious planter of the idea of "riding a winner" and the donor of the ten shillings which started Paul on his winning streak. When Oscar emerges into the foreground as an important character, he serves the purpose of expressing the reader's doubts. "Oscar Cresswell thought about it. 'I'll see the money,' he said." But the joke is on Uncle Oscar, as it will be on the reader if he is too skeptical. When the Leger is run, Oscar bets only two hundred pounds, while the humble and conservative Bassett bets five hundred and the boy a thousand. When their horse wins at the odds of ten to one, Paul is not a bit surprised: " 'You see,' he said, 'I was /545/ absolutely sure of him.' Even Oscar Cresswell had cleared two thousand. 'Look here, son,' he said, 'this sort of thing makes me nervous.' " Lawrence exploits the comic irony of Cresswell's situation, but not to the extent of forfeiting our sympathy with him. So his final bet, on Malabar in the Derby, is made "in spite of himself." And Uncle Oscar is saved to be the speaker of the epitaph for Paul.

Despite the skill and subtlety with which the characters are presented, this is not primarily a story of character. Certain symbols in the story have much more vitality than any of the people in it, and as we have already pointed out, one of the chief characters is not a person but a feeling, a fear, expressed in the unspoken whispers which are as real as breathing. From the very first sentence of the story, "luck" is used as a symbol. In the story as a whole, it seems to be the opposite of, or a substitute for, love. Paul's pursuit of "luck" might be translated as a pursuit of love, if he had been able to understand rightly what he wanted. Then why, if this is what Lawrence means, does he not say so? The answer must be that love is not a concept, to be understood rationally, any more than "luck" is. It must be felt. And he very carefully shows that the absence of love on the part of Paul's mother is not mere failure in kindness, gentleness, or consideration: she is a good mother in these respects, and everybody says so. It is "a hard little place" at the center of her heart; she knows it is there and her children know it is there. "They read it in each other's eyes."

The dialogue between Paul and his mother on the subject of luck is very interesting. Superficially, it is merely a step in the education of the boy; he is learning about an adult idea. But notice how much more Lawrence conveys in this dialogue than is actually expressed in the speeches of the characters; the mother's answers are given "slowly and bitterly," "bitterly," "again with a laugh, but rather bitter." Paul, on the other hand, shows more from his silences than he does from his words. "The boy was /546/ silent for some time." "The boy watched her with unsure eyes." "The child looked at her, to see if she meant it." It is in this dialogue that the boy's hunger for love is betrayed, distorted into the pursuit of luck. But Lawrence is writing a story in which suspense is important, and the revelations here are carefully controlled. Very unobtrusively he prepares for the bitter irony of the end:

"Well, anyhow," he said stoutly, "I'm a lucky person."
"Why?" said his mother, with a sudden laugh.

Paul's last words, as he lies dying, return to this:

"Mother, did I ever tell you? I am lucky."
"No, you never did," said the mother.
But the boy died in the night.

The condemnation of the mother could hardly be more violent, but the irony does not stop here. It continues, to underline Oscar's last words and to force upon us the feeling that Paul was luckier than he knew.

The last three-fourths of the story is devoted to the discovery of Paul's secret; this is done gradually, with some humor, as the character of Uncle Oscar emerges. But at the same time the desperation of the mother increases, the whispering increases so that after the birthday and the mother's receipt of five thousand pounds the voices are screaming. What we have is a building up of Paul's confidence and strength as Uncle Oscar and Bassett seem mere attendants on him, but at the same time the antagonist is growing in strength too, and the way is prepared for the great tragic climax. Lawrence does full justice to the theatrical quality of the scene; the mother's uneasiness at the party, the vague, mysterious noise, the dark bedroom and the sudden blaze of light bringing out the two figures, the boy in his green pyjamas "madly surging" and the mother "as she stood, blonde, in her dress of pale green and crystal, in the doorway." The difference between them is immediately shown in their lines, /547/

"Paul!" she cried. "Whatever are you doing?"
"It's Malabar!" he screamed, in a powerful, strange voice.

Even in all this theatricality the values of the symbols are not lost. Paul's fever and the mother's coldness (now become a coldness of the heart somewhat different from her first state) show us the equivalents in feeling of love and luck.

The Rocking-Horse Winner is not a cheap story with the obvious sentimental moral that life without love is worse than death; it is not a psychological thriller about a boy with extrasensory perception who dies in the act of trying to predict the outcome of the Derby; it is not merely a satire on people who never have enough money, no matter how much they have. Each of these descriptions is wrong because it is incomplete, because it does violence to the particular and individual character of the story. A satisfactory analysis must be one which responds to the way in which Lawrence has woven together character and symbol, theme and plot tension. These elements do not exist separately, they must be seen in relationship to each other. The only reason for taking them apart is to put them back together again and appreciate them more fully.

W. R. Martin

Fancy or Imagination?
"The Rocking-Horse Winner"

D. H. Lawrence's "The Rocking-Horse Winner" appears in several anthologies,[1] and I think it worth while to defend it against the strictures of F. R. Leavis *(D. H. Lawrence: Novelist)* and Graham Hough *(The Dark Sun)*. This can be done by starting with a close analysis of a paragraph to be found near the end of the story:

> Then suddenly she switched on the light, and saw her son, in his green pyjamas, madly surging on the rocking-horse. The blaze of light suddenly lit him up, as he urged the wooden horse, and lit her up, as she stood, blonde, in her dress of pale green and crystal, in the doorway.

The sudden switching on of the light, which "lit him up" and "lit her up, as she stood . . . in the doorway," invites our attention to a heraldically graphic picture that contains the central meaning of the story. That both mother and son are in green marks the culmination of the movement. This is further dramatised and elucidated by "madly" (supported by "surging" and even by "blaze"—a word used several times for the look in the boy's eyes) which is offered in its loose colloquial sense as a description of the boy's motion, but must be taken to refer quite literally to his condition. His madness is an infection caught from his mother, whose hysterical whisper, "There must be more money! There must be more money!" issues finally in the son's "Did I say Malabar, mother? Did I say Malabar?" and prefigures at

*Reprinted from *College English*, XXIV (1962), 64-65, by permission of the National Council of Teachers of English and the author.
[1]The Rinehart Book of Short Stories (1952), D. H. Lawrence: Selected Poetry and Prose (1957), The Portable D. H. Lawrence (1947).

the beginning of the story the frantic iteration in the rocking-horse's motion. Indeed the whisper is echoed by it: "It came whispering from the springs of the still-swaying rocking-horse." To complete the definition of the climax, the mother's "crystal" dress reflects the hardness "at the centre of her heart," and a few lines after our paragraph we are told that the boy's eyes (eyes are an important index throughout) "were like blue stones" and that the mother felt her heart had "turned actually into a stone."

All this is, perhaps, no more than "skilful," which is as far as Hough will go in praise of the story. But "skilful" does less than justice to it, as I hope to show.

Our paragraph refers to the toy as a "rocking-horse"—this is the ninth time it is so called—and in the next line it is a "wooden horse." "Wooden" has appeared twice before, but its definitive connotative /65/ force has not been felt because there has not been this juxtaposition. Now the modulation points with delicately controlled emphasis to the significance of the rocking-horse in the story.

The simple but decisive effect of "wooden" is to make clear a distinction that we now see to have been implicit in the story from the beginning. The real and lively race-horses, whose names—Sansovino, Daffodil, Lancelot, Mirza, Singhalese, Blush of Dawn, Lively Spark—resound insistently through the story, represent with almost crude emblematic clarity the possibilities in a fully lived life and are in ironic contrast to the wooden horse, which, with its "springs," "mechanical gallop" and "arrested prance" is the symbol of the unlived, merely mimetic, life of Paul's parents. The toy horse "doesn't have a name" because it is a nonentity, a substitute: "Till I can have a *real* horse, I like to have *some* sort of animal about." The rocking-horse is seven times referred to simply as the "horse," and this unobtrusively establishes an ironic tension between real life and the unliving imitation.

The tale presents an aspect of the rocking-horse which compels attention. It appears in our paragraph in "madly surging" and "urges." The mother hears a "soundless noise," "something huge, in violent hushed motion"—here again the rocking is linked with the whispering, which "the children could hear all the time, though nobody said it aloud"—and sees him "plunging to and fro." For all this frenzied effort the horse rocks backwards and forwards on the same spot, "still-swaying." Lawrence does not have to score this heavily, but the rocking motion evokes with poetic economy and precision the futility of the parents, whose "prospects never materialised." They buy "splendid and expensive toys" (substitutes, in this story, for *real* things) for

their children; they spend lavishly on themselves in a desperate struggle "to keep up" their social position. Neither the toys nor the social
position give real satisfaction and the parents are condemned to ever
more frantic and meaningless repetition. This is seen in the mother:
she clamours for money, but as soon as she gets the £5,000 she is back
where she was before, wanting more money more desperately. The
parents too are on a rocking-horse, and they are not individuals—like
the wooden horse they have no names—but representatives of a large
section of bourgeois society.

With so much significant meaning so successfully conveyed through
objective correlatives, I cannot agree with Hough that the story is a
product of "fancy not imagination," or share Leavis' exasperation that
it is "so widely regarded (especially in America, it would seem)."
Both Hough and Leavis say that the story is not representative of
Lawrence, but it seems to me to be about, and to dramatize most force-
fully, one of his central concerns: the nature and nemesis of unlived
lives.

William D. Burroughs

No Defense for "The Rocking-Horse Winner"*

W. R. Martin (*CE* Oct. 1962) does not rescue "The Rocking-Horse Winner" from the limitations noted by Leavis and Hough. Furthermore, Gordon and Tate in *The House of Fiction* note the same strictures in the story, although they add that it "approaches technical perfection." That Leavis and Hough have reservations about RHW there is no doubt; however, the grounds for Leavis' reservations are vague: RHW is not representative of Lawrence. Indeed, Professor Martin shows that the story is thematically representative of Lawrence's total works: the unlived life comes through negation of emotions. So, I find Leavis' objections partially answered. On the other hand, Hough is more specific: he substantiates the technical skill of RHW, but he also notes that it is "quite outside the range of Lawrence's usual work."

That the story is technically good, there seems no doubt. This perfection is what Professor Martin defends in the story through cataloguing some of the symbols and imagery for us, at the same time stating that the symbols present the "central meaning of the story." The difficulty with the story comes not with technique, but from what is said. And what Lawrence says in RHW is precisely what he says in his other writings. Another difficulty is Lawrence's unusual plot handling; there is an uneasy feeling about the ending in light of the sample declarative opening (like a fairy tale): "There was a woman who was beautiful, who started with all the advantages, yet she had no luck."

The plot is skillful, but lacks imagination. Lawrence starts his characters at the top, letting them degenerate to poor souls in the denoue-

---

*Reprinted from *College English*, XXIV (1963), 323, by permission of the National Council of Teachers of English and the author.

ment. This arrangement could be tragic if Lawrence had bothered to show some cause-effect for the parents' insistence on social supremacy at Paul's expense; however, the plot is merely the reversal of the fairy-tale climb from rags to riches. It is, although having tragic possibilities, not tragic, but only pathetic. It is this pathos that Hough, Leavis, Gordon and Tate attack.

The emotional appeal goes with Lawrence's insistence that the world should be ruled by emotions (probably an extreme position adopted to make his argument more forceful). His reliance on reader sympathy for Paul, and on reader hate for the parents' materialism, and the dialectic logic of opposites no matter what they represent is strictly emotional.

Moreover, Paul is a romantic, not through interpretation of objective correlatives (a matter of technique in this story): the uncle calls Paul a "romancer" while riding with him in the car. This blunt identification of one of the opposites is balanced by the mother's identification with money, materialism, knowledge, mind, will, intellect. And her symbolic meaning is forthright. In short, the story has a didactic purpose, persuading the reader to accept the dark, the sensual, the blood, the flesh, the senses, the feelings. This plot combination of the fantastic (the boy's insistence on revelation) with the didactic is what critics cannot defend, no matter how much the dialectic is supported by diction.

Professor Martin does not then take up the challenge offered by Leavis and Hough; indeed, no one could. The story is only partially defensible: it is well plotted; the diction, excellent in image, symbol and meaning; and the characters, flat representations of ideas and attitudes. The defense is adequate within its scope, but the value of a short story depends on more than technical perfection.

The lack of other aspects is the objection raised by Leavis, Hough, Gordon and Tate. Fiction depends upon a presentation of life. This presentation is exactly what Lawrence has failed to achieve. In "The Rocking-Horse Winner," he fails to show how his fantastic insistence on the emotional aspects of life can be, or should be, applied to life. So, "The Rocking-Horse Winner," an excellent technical masterpiece, is limited by application of Lawrence's hackneyed didacticism to a pathetic plot of fantasy.

Robert G. Lawrence

Further Notes on D. H. Lawrence's Rocking-Horse*

Professor W. R. Martin wrote perceptively about D. H. Lawrence's "Rocking-Horse Winner," but I was surprised that he made no mention of another significant connotation suggested by the rocking-horse. Surely one of the things which Lawrence had in mind was an allusion to the most famous wooden horse of all: that of Troy. This horse operated to the advantage of its possessors, but the remarkable beast has come down in folklore as a familiar symbol of deception. Paul's wooden horse deceived him in the long run, as he desperately used it as an agent by which he hoped to escape from his problems; yet it did no more than lead him more deeply into a trap.

Only a scholar better versed than I in the byways of psychology can speak with authority on this second characteristic of the rocking-horse. Did Lawrence intend Paul's intense interest in the toy to represent a regression further into childhood rather than a movement toward adulthood and its problems? The answer to the query depends on Paul's age, which Lawrence never specified; however, the mother says, "Surely, you're too big for a rocking-horse!" and Uncle Oscar remarks, "You're not a very little boy any longer." Paul, evidently the eldest of the children, is out of the nursery and seems to have given up his teddy bear; he is also old enough to study Latin and Greek under tutors at home.

Neither of these suggestions contradicts the point of view of Professor Martin, but both serve to reinforce the unity which the rocking-horse contributes to the story.

*Reprinted from *College English*, XXIV (1963), 324, by permission of the National Council of Teachers of English and the author.

57

Frank O'Connor

Poe and "The Rocking-Horse Winner"*

The development of a short-story writer who ceases to be a short-story writer and becomes something else is fascinating, at least to another short-story writer. Joyce, as I have said, stops dead and then resumes his work with autobiographical fantasias, written in a style that becomes more and more elaborate and in which the submerged population of the short stories becomes liberated into figures from classical mythology. Lawrence, the intuitive artist, never ceases to write stories, but their quality changes. His style, like that of most intuitive artists, had always been swift and certain, though in his haste he might often have used conjunctions to begin his sentences and exclamation points to end them. In his later work the style becomes more exasperating with its "ands," "buts," "sos," and "whereases" and hysterical with exclamation points and italics, and side by side with this his characters were changing as Joyce's changed, from the /153/ submerged population of the English Midlands to the symbolic figures of the English society papers — lords and ladies, wealthy businessmen, American millionaires and their families. *Lady Chatterley's Lover* is only Louisa's lover in "The Daughters of the Vicar" but with all the sense of actuality left out. In the form of the novel this change is intolerable — a novel, no matter how fantastic, must have some sense of actuality. In the stories and *nouvelles* the withdrawal of the sense of actuality draws them gradually closer to the condition of tales — nearer to Pushkin and Poe, farther from Chekhov and Maupassant. They are excellent tales; that sense of the

*Reprinted from *The Lonely Voice: A Study of the Short Story* (Cleveland and New York: The World Publishing Company, 1965), pp. 153-155, by permission. A Meridian Book. Copyright © 1962, 1963 by Frank O'Connor. Title supplied by the editor.

miraculous which is in Lawrence's work from the beginning saves
them from becoming mere exercises in the occult, but no set of standards that will apply to Chekhov and Maupassant can be applied to
them.

Am I wrong in suspecting that something about the change in his
work can be attributed to his English upbringing? Both in him and
Coppard there is a feeling of social inadequacy which makes them a
little too anxious to get away from their backgrounds and meditate
too much upon the sheer beauty of an independent income. Lawrence
managed to persuade his admirers that the only thing he really cared
for was a sexual potency that smoothed out abstraction and fastidious-
ness, but this was one of the major achievements of a major yarn-
spinner because he really loved rank and money more than most
people and to him sex was merely a convenient method of ironing
out the inequalities imposed on him by his birth. No doubt, as a
serious prophet he deplored the worship of money, but anyone who
reads "The Rock- /154/ inghorse Winner" without wondering ex-
citedly exactly how much the neurotic small boy will accumulate
through riding his rockinghorse and visualizing the winners of the
classic races before Nemesis catches up with him must be a critical St.
Francis of Assisi. No doubt the child's death is a very proper punishment for his family's preoccupation with money, though why he
rather than his family should be punished is something of a problem,
but at the same time eighty thousand pounds — three hundred thousand dollars in the exchange of the period — is handsome compensa-
tion. My only doubt is whether the story should not have been written
by Poe in his *Tales of Mystery and Imagination.*

James G. Hepburn

Disarming and Uncanny Visions

Freudian literary criticism has long suffered from success. The reaction against it finds one form of expression in Stanley Edgar Hyman's *The Armed Vision:* "The obvious limitation of traditional Freudian literary analysis is that only one study can be written, since every additional one would turn out to say the same thing. Ernest Jones could do a beautiful job of finding the underlying Oedipus complex in *Hamlet,* but had he gone on to analyze *Lear* or *A Midsummer Night's Dream* or the *Sonnets* he would have found to his surprise that they reflected Shakespeare's Oedipus complex too . . . A criticism that can only say . . . [one thing] turns out not to be saying very much."[1] Jones, of course, was not surprised to find the Oedipus complex in *Hamlet,* since Freud in *The Interpretation of Dreams* had already intimated what the fruits of the inquiry would be. But that is neither here nor there; when we descend from Jones on *Hamlet* to, say, Daniel Schneider on *Death of a Salesman* we see as Hyman does. With hardly any effort Schneider uncovers an Oedipus complex, which for him provides the explanation for both the play's undoubted success and its supposed greatness.[2] On such a basis Sir Lawrence Olivier's lurid film version of *Hamlet* is Shakespeare improved, and any popular story that panders to sexual anxieties merits the attention of the ages. One doesn't say very much when one merely points out the Oedipus complex in a work — no more, certainly, than when

[1]New York, 1948, p. 166.
[2]*The Psychoanalyst and the Artist* (New York, 1950), pp. 346-55.

*Reprinted from "Disarming and Uncanny Visions; Freud's 'The Uncanny' with Regard to Form and Content in Stories by Sherwood Anderson and D. H. Lawrence," *Literature and Psychology,* IX (Winter, 1959), 9-12, by permission.

one merely points out archetypal patterns, myths, organic metaphors, and great themes.

Not that most of us would care to abandon viewpoints that sometimes bring us closer to art than we have been before. To read Jones on *Hamlet* after reading Goethe, Schlegel, Bradley, and Eliot is to come into light from twilight; here is the objective correlative clearly seen. And not that Hyman is right in assuming that the analysis of *Lear* must repeat that of *Hamlet*. Freud himself, if not Jones, proceeds from *Hamlet* to *Lear, Macbeth,* and other plays without repeating himself. He does so the easy way, by discussing other phychological matters than the Oedipus complex. But he could have done so the hard way. In his preface to Theodore Reik's *Ritual* he remarks that "through the elaboration of this complex into the most manifold variants, distortions and disguises, the poet seeks to elucidate his most personal attitude to this effective theme.[3] The Freudian critic is concerned with literary strategies as well as with hidden subject-matter, with form as well as with content. A study of the Oedipus complex in several of Shakespeare's plays need be no more repetitious than a study of the theme of the American in Europe in Henry James' novels.

Freudian literary criticism is inherently rash; it is not inherently simplistic. Up until now it has concerned itself primarily with the unravelling of hidden subjects and meanings, along with the corollary unravelling of motives; its more significant and complex task — as with psychoanalysis itself — is the analysis of strategies, of form. Freud himself in his writings on literature emphasizes matters of content, but he does suggest approaches to the study of form. One of his little-known essays, "The Uncanny,"[4] is interesting for the variety of its suggestiveness.

In "Death in the Woods" and "The Rocking-Horse Winner" Sherwood Anderson and D. H. Lawrence have created stories of remarkably delicate power. There is some accounting for this power; it appears to lie in part in an analysis of a quality they share: the evocation of a sense of the uncanny.

"Death in the Woods" is in most respects a clear enough account of an old woman's death, upon which the author imposes a philosophical meaning. The woman had possibly been the child of an illegitimate

[3]London, 1931, p. 8. For Freud's discussion of other Shakespearian plays see "Some Character Types Met with in Psychoanalytic Work" and "The Theme of the Three Caskets" in his *Collected Papers,* IV (London, 1925).

[4]*Collected Papers,* IV, 368-407.

passion; when she was young she was bound into service; as a young woman she was the helpless victim of sexual approaches by her employer; in marriage she served her husband sexually; throughout her life she fed animals and bought and cooked food for men; now as she dies in the woods with food slung on her back she one last time feeds her dogs. Anderson comments within the story: "The woman who died was one destined to feed animal life . . . She was feeding animal life before she was born, as a child, as a young woman working on the farm of the German, after she married, when she grew old and when she died . . . . A thing so complete has its own beauty."

The problems of the story that present themselves to the reader are few but crucial; they concern both form and content: structure, strategy, intent, and description. First, why does Anderson tell the story in the fashion that he does? Why does he emphasize at the outset that "it is a story," later that he is puzzled by his ability to reconstruct the far past, and towards the end that his "real story" is actually pieced together from miscellaneous unrelated fragments of his own experience? The obvious answer is that all of this is so, and a glance through his Memoirs[5] will confirm the opinion. But such synthesis is the method of most stories, whose art, however, is to conceal what Anderson reveals. Then perhaps the story was carelessly written, or the narrative method was accidentally developed. /10/ To the reader who regards the story highly and who knows that this was probably the most carefully written of Anderson's stories, labored over for years and revised several times, such explanations will not suffice.

Secondly, Anderson seems to reject the literary rule that meaning is better implied than baldly stated. In the quoted passage on the beauty of the old woman's life, as well as at several other junctures, he apparently gives away what properly should be hinted at, forces upon the circumstances what should emanate from it. And yet the reader does not feel that Anderson has failed. Why is this so?

There are, additionally, two problems of detail. When the old woman lies freezing to death in the woods, the dogs circling before her, the reader is led to suspect that her end may be gruesome. The dogs have been described as gaunt, starved; they have ranged about the woods chasing rabbits; now they are "excited about something" and seem to Anderson to revive their wolfish ancestry. One by one the dogs come up to the dying woman, look into her face, their red tongues hanging out. But when she is dead, the dogs assault her only

---

[5]New York, 1942, pp. 40-44, 310-12.

for the food on her back; they do not touch her body. The reader perhaps feels misled, if not dissatisfied; he asks with what legitimacy Anderson hints at an attack upon the woman's body which does not occur.

The other problem concerns the physical description of the woman. She is called an "old woman," although she is about forty. (Anderson's remark on her age is ambiguous; it is certain, though, from other evidence that she cannot be more than a year or two above forty.) Anderson explains that she has become bent and sick with her labor and poverty. Then when she lies dead she loses her agedness. Part of her body has been exposed as the dogs have torn at the food on her back, and she seems to the hunter who discovers her "a beautiful young girl" and to the storyteller, who comes upon the scene later, "some charming young girl." If the reader is surprised when after the picture of a truly old woman has been well established he is informed of her comparatively young age, he is nonplussed by her final transfiguration into a lovely young girl — once again after the image of an old woman has re-established itself.

To answer these questions it is necessary first to examine the main image of the story, the dead woman lying in the woods. She lies prone, her body exposed to the waist. Upon the arrival of the townspeople, the storyteller as a young boy among them, she is turned over for identification. The boy, who has never before seen a woman's body, sees "everything" and experiences a "strange mystical feeling," apparently similar to the "uncanny" sensation of the hunter who had first discovered her. Of course the boy does not see "everything"; he sees only the woman's breasts, which are never mentioned. One thinks then of the meaning of the story given by Anderson: this is the woman who all her life has fed men. Yet Anderson has again left unmentioned, has nowhere overtly suggested, the basic manner in which this woman — all women, for he generalizes — feeds man: at her breast. But if one reflects upon the woman's nakedness in the woods, it is possible to infer that the entire scene covertly concerns breast-feeding and hence that the main image of the story concerns the point that Anderson has apparently ignored — his art being to conceal. The inference requires some hazardous leaps: the reader has suspected that the dogs will attack the woman's body for food — as once the storyteller or reader took his mother's breast to his mouth for food; but the dogs leave the woman's body unharmed — as the storyteller or reader so left his mother's breast; all that the dogs want is the food on her back — as the storyteller or reader wanted only the food on her front. Perhaps these suggestions are extravagant. Then consider that the old woman who feeds the dogs is a young-old woman; and the woman who feeds her child is a young, "beautiful," "charming" woman, whose act the child consciously forgets and who is old, sexless when the child as an adolescent re-discovers the female breasts as sexual objects. The storyteller tells a lie (Anderson would say that lying is his function); he has once before seen a woman so exposed.

The two problems of detail are perhaps tentatively cleared up. The intent and actions of the dogs symbolize the intent and actions of the infant, and the young-old woman is compounded of the nursing mother who is remembered unconsciously and the graying mother known consciously. Anderson's main strategy seems to appear: he is telling not, a story that is easy to understand, with a meaning flatly stated at the end, but a story that he may not comprehend and whose paramount meaning he can only suggest. His final words are, "I have been impelled to *try* [emphasis added] to tell the simple story over again." And his narrative form may seem a deliberate means of conveying to the reader the sense of mystery, of meaning for which there are only scattered clues, of something profound and general implied by some isolated occurrences, of a memory "like music heard from far off" that reverberates in recesses of the mind. Or the form may be an unconscious acknowledgement of the intractability of his material. Or it is both.

The powerful element of the uncanny remains unexplored. It is unlikely that the reader has much if any sense of the uncanny in the woods scene, but the term *uncanny* is used twice in its presentation and to good purpose. The first time it is employed to suggest the hunter's emotion upon finding the body; his emotion links to the storyteller's feelings upon seeing the woman. Secondly, the word appears in the storyteller's reference to an occurrence in his young manhood, when he had an experience with dogs similar to the old woman's. The uncanny points to two things then: the uncovering of the female body: specifically the breasts, and the attack of dogs. Here Freud's essay becomes useful. In it he offers the following psychological stages for sensing the uncanny. (1) Any emotion, whatever its quality, is transformed by repression into morbid anxiety. (2) Any new situation that recalls an old one whose emotion (affect) is repressed will arouse anxiety. (3) This anxiety will have the quality of uncanniness (etymologically "the unknown," psychoanalytically the unknown-known—that is, repressed from conscious knowledge) when either (a) infantile complexes, such as cas /11/ tration, Oedipus, and womb fantasies, are revived, or (b) ontogenetically primitive beliefs, such as animism, magic, and omnipotence of thought seem once more to be confirmed. Freud's analysis, joined with our interpretation of the story, explains the evocation of the sense of the uncanny. The infantile complex central to the story is a breast fantasy; the storyteller as he sees a naked woman supposedly for the first time recalls, on a preconscious level, the repressed infantile relationship to the mother in its complex of hunger, oral eroticism, and oral aggression; he senses the uncanny.

The uncanniness of the dogs attacking the woman's body repeats the uncanniness of the exposure of the breasts; the uncanniness of their attack may carry additionally the overtone of the repressed genital desires of the child — "repressed" here by the dogs, which, like the child, take only food. The new implication is supported by the uncanniness of the storyteller's experience as a young man, when the dogs attack him. The attack here would be castrative, and the uncanniness would be the recollection of the infantile fear — the recollection coming at a time when the revival of sexual activity after latency revives the threat that accompanies infantile sexual desires.

Since a threat of castration is primarily a threat by the father and since the attack upon the woman suggests more than a child's desire ("The dog thrust his face close to her face. His red tongue was hanging out"), an adult male is of some importance to the atmosphere of the story.[6] He is the sexual partner of the mother who feeds men: he is, presumably, both the German employer and Jake Grimes, the old woman's husband. The dual image can perhaps be referred to broad aspects of father-son relationships. The German's brutal aggressiveness reflects a child's characteristic envy or awe of the father's sexual prowess and a child's common delusion of his mother's victimization. Jake Grimes, on the other hand, although like the German a man to fear, a drunkard, a horse thief, a man who contains violence, displays in the story no obvious sexual lust for the old woman; Anderson mentions that later in life the old woman did not feed him "in a certain way." Grimes perhaps represents the father who threatens not the mother but the child, he who punishes the child's sexual activity by castration.

If the reader himself has any sense of the uncanny while reading the story, it is not at either the point when the woman's body is turned over or the reminiscence of the storyteller's experience of

[6]Irving Howe remarks, "The old woman seems an image of the overwhelmed feminine victim, for even the dogs that attend her are male." *Sherwood Anderson* (New York, 1951), p. 166.

young manhood; it occurs in one or two descriptive passages, the first
of the cold, bare, and silent woodlands, the woman dozing and the
dogs circling, and the second of the same scene after the hunter has
found the body. Two questions arise: what is the source of uncanniness here, and why should the sensation at one juncture belong only
to the storyteller and at another to — presumably — both storyteller
and reader? Freud in his article has an answer to the first. Having
noted that silence, solitude, and darkness are frequent scenic com-
ponents of uncanny situations, he suggests their appropriateness
through being "elements in the production of that infantile morbid
anxiety from which the majority of human beings have never become
quite free."[7] Along with coldness and snow, silence, solitude, and
darkness constitute Anderson's scenes. They revivify the actual uncanny situations that the other elements of the story call to mind.

The other question has two answers. First of all, Anderson slights
description, emotion, and atmosphere at the points of exposure of the
woman's body and his young manhood experience, whereas he more
carefully builds and sustains the scenes that do evoke uncanniness.
Secondly, the exposure and young manhood scenes are experiences of
the storyteller, whose personal role is insignificant and from whom
the reader stands apart; contrastingly, the uncanny scenes are clearly
intended for the reader's mind and imagination. In his article, Freud
offers several illustrations of comparable restrictions upon the evocation of the uncanny.

D. H. Lawrence's story is a knottier problem than Anderson's. A
favorite of the anthologists (it was first published in an anthology of
stories of the uncanny), it has nevertheless received little scrutiny and
has resisted scrutiny well; it seems especially designed to teach hu-
mility to critics. Harry T. Moore in his *Life and Works of D. H.
Lawrence* acknowledges that the power of the story cannot be ade-
quately explained in terms of its depiction of the "money neurosis" of
modern society, but he is unable to get behind its "contagious excitement," "inescapable doom," and "horror."[8] Robert Gorham Davis
invokes myth and lore: " 'The Rocking-Horse Winner' is a parable
on the money lusts of modern society, but it draws its magic from
very ancient sources. Hobbyhorses are very common in folklore, and
there are accounts of rituals in which their riders rocked themselves
into a trance in order to attain powers of prophecy."[9] Davis doesn't

---

[7]P. 407.
[8]New York, 1951, pp. 278-79.
[9]In his anthology *Ten Modern Masters* (New York, 1953), p. 388.

explain where the ancient source gets *its* magic and power and by
what apparatus Lawrence's story draws upon the past. Even less help-
fully Caroline Gordon and Allen Tate in *The House of Fiction* affirm
that Paul "has invoked strange gods"; he is "in the grip of a supernatural power."[10] From the psychoanalytic viewpoint the story has
been analyzed as a childhood problem of homosexuality and masturbation, but the interpretation seems decidedly less meaningful than
an analysis of overt themes. The most recent approach to the story, by
W. D. Snodgrass, attempts a synthesis of several viewpoints; it establishes — in some respects quite successfully — an interrelationship
among the themes of money, masturbation, and adult love; but in the
process the story gets lost: Paul emerges at one point as "a symbol of
civilized man . . ., the scientist, teacher, theorist, who must always
know about /12/ the outside world so that he can manipulate it. . . ."[11]

The story defies sufficient explication. However, insofar as its power
is related to the sense of the uncanny that Lawrence evokes, it can be
approached in terms of Freud's analysis: (1) The uncanny as, in part,
the unknown-known is intimated in several ways in the story. There
are the open secrets of the household, not spoken but read in the
eyes: that at the core of the mother's heart there is no love; that the
family needs money. There are the personal knowledge, feeling, and
action kept from others: that Paul bets and rides his horse to win;
something that his mother withholds when Paul asks her why she is
unlucky. More importantly, there are the mysterious cognitions:
Paul's power of prophecy, when he "knows"; his mother's divination
as she comes into his room at the end. All of this suggests elements of,
or the atmosphere of, uncanny situations. (2) The uncanny, in one of
its two aspects ("Death in the Woods" illustrates the other), takes us
back to primitive ways of thinking. "The Rocking-Horse Winner"
offers three important categories: (a) animism — the rocking-horse
as a real horse, (b) omnipotence of thought — predicting the winners,
(c) fatalism — lucky and unlucky persons. (3) The sense of the uncanny does not arise automatically from primitive thinking. The
frank abandonment of reality in the fairy tale and the frank indulgence in childish ways of thought will not produce a sense of the
uncanny. For although the fairy tale may recall infantile ways of
thought, it does not seem to confirm those ways of thought. Uncanniness arises only when "the writer pretends to move in the world of
common reality . . ., takes advantage, as it were, of our supposedly

[10]New York, 1950, p. 351.
[11]"A Rocking-Horse: The Symbol, the Pattern, The way to Live," *Hudson Review*, XI, (1958), 191-200.

surmounted superstitiousness . . ., deceives us into thinking that he is giving us the sober truth, and then after all oversteps the bounds of possibility."[12] Lawrence's story meets Freud's conditions, although it achieves a more delicate balance than Freud envisions. For it possesses very nearly the quality of the fairy tale: "There was a woman who was beautiful, who started with all the advantages, yet she had no luck." This quality—if one accepts Freud's conditions—constantly threatens failure in the evocation of the uncanny; it constantly weighs against the realism of the story. Perhaps Lawrence's major triumph in the story is that he achieves uncanniness at such a risk.

Perhaps. But one thinks that the fairy-tale quality of the story has its own virtues; it is the basis of the story's beautiful economy. Single explanations will not suffice. The Freudian critic may feel entitled to change "draws its magic from very ancient sources" to "draws its magic — under restricted conditions — from childhood sources," but he has not thereby explained "The Rocking-Horse Winner." He might go further by examining the style and tone of some other Lawrence stories for their fairy-tale qualities and asking himself how they serve as literary strategies. Here would be a problem to sink his teeth into. The consequence might be an armed vision.

E. W. Tedlock, Jr.

Values and "The Rocking-Horse Winner"*

"The Rocking-Horse Winner," probably the most frequently anthologized of Lawrence's stories, is a wonderfully sustained, shocking exploration of the vital, human cost of the abstract value of getting on in the world. It is rare among Lawrence's mature stories in its revelation of his great warmth for children, so clear in his early work. In the opening exposition, the reflexive play of the value terms is like a seed from which the story must develop a life or death struggle. The tone, that of the fairy tale, at once turns the social-psychological aspect of the situation towards the archetypical.

There was a woman who was beautiful, who started with all the advantages, yet she had no luck. She married for love, and the love turned to dust. She had bonny children, yet she felt they had been thrust upon her, and she could not love them. They looked at her coldly, as if they were finding fault with her. And hurriedly she felt she must cover up some fault in herself. Yet what it was that she must cover up she never knew. Nevertheless, when her children were present, she always felt the centre of her heart go hard.

As Paul pursues his mother's love through luck on his rocking horse, that simple simulacrum of the natural that is so real to a child's imagination turns into a frantically galloping perversity. The boy's eyes become increasingly hard and cold, like those of the imitation horse, until near the end they are "like blue stones." And when his

---

*Reprinted from *D. H. Lawrence: Artist and Rebel* (Albuquerque: University of New Mexico Press, 1963), pp. 209-210, by permission. Title supplied by the editor.

69

mother, her burst /210/ of terrible anxiety confirmed, feels that her heart has turned into a stone, the rhythmic terror of Lawrence's apprehension of the dehumanization of life comes to rest like the last stroke of a hammer.

On the realistic, psychological side, he creates in detail the ambiguous social passion of the parents that has replaced love, the child's sensitiveness to adult anxiety, and his picking up of a false clue to action from the mother's vague identification of lack of luck and money with her empty life. The muddle of values is revealed in such verbal confusions as the boy's identification of his uncle's "filthy lucre" with "filthy lucker." Characteristically, though all of the adults are involved in Lawrence's indictment, it is pronounced by the least respectable, the gambler uncle.

W. S. Marks III

The Psychology of The Uncanny in Lawrence's "The Rocking-Horse Winner"

"The Rocking-Horse Winner," one of a group of Lawrence's tales of the supernatural, appeared in October, 1926, in Cynthia Asquith's *The Ghost Book*.[1] In 1925, the year of Lawrence's arrival in England from a three-year sojourn in North and Central America, the Hogarth Press had published Joan Riviere's translation of *Papers on Applied Psycho-Analysis*, the fourth volume of Freud's *Collected Papers*.[2] Just one year previously Boni and Liveright had published her standard translation of *A General Introduction to Psychoanalysis*, which had already gone through two earlier English translations in 1920 and 1922. The period of Lawrence's brief return to London marks what might be considered the apogee of the Freudian vogue in Bloomsbury. His American trip, moreover, had coincided with the remarkable rise of Freud's infant science in this country. Bracketing his stay at Taos Lawrence had completed two of a projected three amateur essays in psychoanalytic theory with *Psychoanalysis and The Unconscious* and its continuation, *Fantasia of The Unconscious*, where Freud's contributions toward an understanding of the unconscious are curtly acknowledged in the preface. Lawrence's direct references to Freud and the Viennese School, as well as statements in his letters, generally give a deliberate misimpression that he found Freud's ideas rather

*Reprinted from *Modern Fiction Studies*, XI, No. 4 (1965-66), 381-392, by permission. *Modern Fiction Studies*, © 1965-66 by Purdue Research Foundation, Lafayette, Indiana.

[1]This group includes "The Borderline," "The Last Laugh," and "Glad Ghosts." For a brief account of *The Ghost Book* see Harry T. Moore, *The Intelligent Heart* (Baltimore, 1960), p. 431.

[2]Sigmund Freud, *Collected Papers*, 5 vols. (London, 1924-50). Citations to Freud's papers parenthesized in the the text will be to the volumes of this edition.

crude and uninteresting.[3] While largely disclaiming Freud's influence on his work as an amateur scientist, however, Lawrence the professional writer seems to have made at least selective use of both Freud's lectures in *A General Introduction to Psychoanalysis* and a number of the classic case histories in the *Collected Papers*. Among these papers, "A Special Type of Object-Choice," "Obsessive Acts and Religious Practices," "The /382/ 'Uncanny,'" "From the Neurosis of Demoniacal Possession in The Seventeenth Century," "The History of An Infantile Neurosis," and "A Phobia in A Five Year Old Boy" provide the most illuminating analogies with Paul's behavior in "The Rocking-Horse Winner." Moreover, I believe Freud's theoretical conclusions drawn from these analyses help to integrate the various psycho-sexual, supernatural, and historical aspects of the boy's "tragedy." Finally, Freud's papers also contain valuable suggestions toward the parodic style of this story, which has generally seemed a remarkable departure from the usual to Lawrence's critics.[4]

While he remains open to charges of aesthetic insensitivity, or at least narrow mindedness, Freud must be credited with pointing out a variety of literary implications in the neurotic behavior of his patients. In "Obsessive Acts and Religious Practices" (1907) he remarks that obsessional actions, since they parody ritual, furnish "a tragic-comic travesty of private religion," and may therefore be interpreted symbolically and historically as well as literally. Theorizing along lines to be more exhaustively pursued by Rank and Jung, Freud asserts that the "primal phantasies" of neurotics are symbolic condensations of racial history. In his Vienna lectures he speculates ". . . that all that to-day is narrated in analysis in the form of phantasy,... was in prehistoric periods of the human family a reality; and that the child in phantasy simply fills out the gaps in its true prehistoric experience."[5] The parody of "The Rocking-Horse Winner"

---

[3]In "Lawrence's Quarrel With Freud," Frederick J. Hoffman and Harry T. Moore, eds., *The Achievement of D. H. Lawrence* (Okla., 1953), pp. 106-130, Mr. Hoffman shows that Lawrence only took a conversational interest in psychoanalysis until 1921-22; when he began to study the methods of Freud and his disciples in earnest.

[4]Graham Hough considers the story "quite outside Lawrence's usual range," while Harry T. Moore finds it uncharacteristically "acidic." For their respective comments on "The Rocking-Horse Winner" see *The Dark Sun* (New York, 1957), p. 188, and The *Intelligent Heart*, pp. 429-31. On the other hand, W. D. Snodgrass has ably argued that this tale expresses the essence of Lawrence's doctrine and his literary genius. In "A Rocking-Horse Winner: The Symbol, The Pattern, The Way To Live," reprinted in Mark Spilka, ed., *D. H. Lawrence: A Collection of Critical Essays* (New Jersey, 1963), pp. 117-126, Mr. Snodgrass anticipates my own analysis by stressing Paul's Oedipal behavior pattern, but without reference to Freud's relevant studies of autoerotic fantasies and uncanny behavior in children.

results from just such a translation of primitive myth and ritual to the bourgeois nursery as Freud accomplished in establishing the existence of the Oedipus complex. The earlier fiction of Thomas Mann, Kafka, and Joyce in some cases anticipate Freud in exploiting the dramatic and symbolic possibilities of modern man's fantasy life, amply showing that the modern short story and the psychoanalytical movement were concurrently developing a similar body of ideas.

In Freud's classic cases the daydream or fantasy, since it is usually /383/ Oedipal and autoerotic,[6] becomes increasingly a cause for guilt feelings, furtiveness, and at last pathological fear of retribution, often manifesting itself as an animal phobia. Such is the progress of little Hans, the protagonist of "A Phobia in A Five Year Old Boy." At one point Hans, whose behavior Freud drolly compares with that of the Adult lover, conceives the fantastic scheme of giving a guard 50,000 florins to let him ride on a truck. Freud suggests that this "... almost sounds like a plan of buying his mother from his father, part of whose power, of course, lay in his wealth." Fearing punishment from the father, Hans develops a castration complex linked with a pathological fear of horses. Such totemic animals, Freud believes, represent surrogate parents, toward which the boy directs a frustrated love for his real father and mother. Essentially agreeing on this point, Jung, in *The Psychology of the Unconscious* (1916), interprets the horses ridden in dreams as especially common symbols for the libido in a state of repression. Fixated at a narcissistic stage of development, Paul's libido is precisely objectified in the rocking-horse. Lawrence's young hero gives a first indication of his symptomatic preoccupation with riding (which later becomes obsessional) when he asks his mother: "... why don't we keep a car of our own? Why do we always use uncle's, or else a taxi?" Her reply, "Because

---

[5] Sigmund Freud, *A General Introduction to Psychoanalysis* (New York, 1953), p. 380.

[6] "An unsuspectedly large proportion of obsessive actions," Freud writes, "are found to be disguised repetitions and modifications of masturbation, admittedly the only uniform act which accompanies all the varied flights of sexual phantasy"—*A General Introduction To Psychoanalysis*, pp. 318-319. One of these obsessive actions which conceal Oedipal guilt and the repressed desire to masturbate is compulsive gambling. Freud discusses this pertinent subject in "Dostoievsky and Parricide" (1928), *Collected Papers*, V, 237 f., where he draws on three earlier books Lawrence may have known or heard about: Jolan Neufeld, *Dostojewski, Skizze zu seiner Psychoanalyze, Internationaler psychoanalytischer Verlag*, Vol. IV (1923); René Fülop-Miller, *Die Krisis in Dostojewsky's Leben (Dostojewsky am Roulette)* (Muenchen, 1925); and René Fülop-Miller and Friedrich Eckstein, eds., *Lebenserinnerungen der Gattin Dostojewskys* (Muenchen, 1925). This last, the diaries of Anna Dostoevskaya, is especially interesting where it describes her husband's notorious penchant for the gaming tables as "diabolical possession."

we're poor members of the family," fatally impresses Paul with the
association between money and the power to "ride," precipitating
his short but sensational career as a gambler.

Narrowing and extending the nineteenth century's philosophic version of the infant, Freud interpreted the child as a symbolic man,
but drew darker inferences than the early Romantics concerning
his infantile tendencies to superstitious, ritualistic, and inspired behavior. As he emerges from the *Collected Papers*, the Oedipal child
appears as the miniature hero of a fantasy situation called the
"family romance," a mythic drama in which the stock events of knight
errantry are used symbolically to disguise the child's suppressed long-
ing to woo his mother and to replace her husband. Paul would be
/384/ specifically indulging in "the rescue phantasy,"[7] in which the
child imagines he is saving a princess (his mother) from some terrible
danger (in Paul's case, financial insecurity). Paul's ability to make
lucky predictions by riding himself into a trance on his totemic
hobbyhorse is principally suggested by Freud's paper "The 'Uncanny,'" where this phenomenon is defined as a product of narcissistic regression to a primitive belief in animism:

> Our analysis of instances of the uncanny has led us back to the
> old, animistic conception of the universe, which was character-
> ized by the idea that the world was peopled with the spirits of
> human beings, and by the narcissistic overestimation of subjec-
> tive mental processes (such as the belief in the omnipotence of
> thoughts, the magical practices based upon this belief, the care-
> fully proportioned distribution of magical powers or 'mana'
> among various outside persons and things), as well as by all those
> other figments of the imagination with which man, in the unre-
> stricted narcissism of that stage of development, strove to with-
> stand the inexorable laws of reality. It would seem as though
> each one of us has been through a phase of individual develop-
> ment corresponding to that animistic stage in primitive men, that
> none of us has traversed it without preserving certain traces of it
> which can be reactivated, and that everything which now strikes
> us as 'uncanny' fulfills the condition of stirring those vestiges of
> animistic mental activity within us and bringing them to expres-
> sion. (IV, 393-94)

Paul's self-destructive act of rocking comes under the heading of
Freud's *repetition-compulsion*: ". . . a principle powerful enough to
over-rule the pleasure-principle, lending to certain aspects of the mind

---

[7]Described by Freud in "Contributions To the Psychology of Love. A Special Type
of Choice and Object made by Men," *Collected Papers*, IV, pp. 192-202.

their daemonic character, and still very clearly expressed in the tendencies of small children" (IV, 391).

In the more extended "From The History of An Infantile Neurosis" the patient passes through several phases which provide still further and more illuminating analogies with Paul's Oedipal pattern. In the first phase we have the familiar animal phobia, involving here a deathly fear of wolves, and "uncanny feelings" about horses, which the boy, suppressing a desire to masturbate, imagines he is beating. In adolescence the boy enters a new phase as his affection suddenly polarizes toward the father. During this period the boy conceives a masochistic desire to become the passive instrument of his father's pleasure. Identifying himself with Christ, he becomes ascetically pious, obsessively ceremonial, and even mystical in his reverence of God the Father. Under the influence of a revered tutor, however, still another apparent reversal takes place as the boy adopts his teacher's scorn of religion. The patient hereupon enters a militaristic phase with overtones of nationalism, conceiving "an enthusiasm for /385/ military affairs, for uniforms and horses," which became "food for continual daydreams." These chivalric fantasies, Freud notes, "correspond exactly to the legends by means of which a nation that has become great and proud tries to conceal the insignificance and failures of its beginnings." Freud's comment, if we accept W. D. Snodgrass's suggestion that Paul's victories at the track are meant to parody British annexations in India,[8] seems to provide another key to Lawrence's satirical intention. While the story implies a criticism of British colonial imperialism through the names of the horses Singhalese, Malabar, and Mirza, the horse "Lancelot" does not fit this category, but suggests an ironic parallel between the boy's Oedipal "chivalry" and that of Arthurian romance with its secular idealization of woman. Uncle Oscar calls the boy, significantly, "a young romancer." Quite possibly Paul's "riding" also parodies St. George, the hero of British national myth whose prowess is celebrated in the English Mummers' Play by the riding of hobbyhorses. On his father's death, Freud's patient enters the last phase of his neurosis when he receives a substantial inheritance. The young man looks upon this money as filth or faeces—a poor substitute for his living father. Under Freud's guidance the patient finally comes to realize that both God and his tutor were only poor surrogates for the real father he had always loved. In "The Rocking-Horse Winner," we have a similar substitution of money for primitive phallic values and paternal authority in the home. Also, since medieval chivalry

---

[8]Snodgrass, p. 121.

was a Christian institution, it is possible to see further parallels between the masochistic piety of Freud's neurotic young man and the
self-laceration of Lawrence's Paul. Thus Lawrence's tiny hero becomes
a type of the historic Christian martyr, as well as the Oedipal hero of
Antique tragedy.

A typical Lawrentian protagonist, young Paul, like Paul Morel and
Gerald Crich, is kept from maturity by an Oedipal attachment to the
mother. Through her baleful influence Paul forsakes the phallic gods
of the patriarchal household, cleaving to the obscene idols of the
matriarch. Ultimately, he becomes a scapegoat who atones for the sins
of his house—the material, social, and intellectual ambitions that
corrupt normal affection, dislocate the proper authority of the father,
and disintegrate the moral ties of the family, replacing them with the
cash-nexus. Paul's death, we may assume, finally stills the haunting
whisper, "There must be more money!" When Uncle Oscar asks the
boy what he intends doing with his mysterious fortune, he naively
replies: "I started it for my mother. /386/ She said she had no luck,
because father is unlucky, so I thought if I was lucky, it might stop
whispering—I *hate* our house for whispering." Lawrence uses the
word "luck" ironically here to connote sexual as well as material
gratification, thus hinting at an underlying cause of the mother's
bitterness at her husband's failure to assume a natural masculine
authority. Rather than explain her sexual disappointment to the boy,
she quite understandably tells Paul that "luck" (which the boy ironically confuses with his Uncle's phrase "filthy lucre") means money.[9]
The story thus depends on a radical "failure of definition" arising out
of the kind of verbal ambiguity Freud delighted in exploring as a
clue to the repressed life of his patients.

In "The Rocking-Horse Winner" Paul's attempts to control the
family's external fortunes correspond with similar instances of uncanny powers which Freud discovered as illusions of the primitive
mind and which he associated with narcissism. Freud was led to
investigate primitive behavior when he continued to notice the
analogies it provided with the regressive tendencies of the modern
neurotic. As in *Faustus and Macbeth*,[10] works Freud specifically

---

[9]The role of the phrase "filthy lucre" in the psychoanalytical interpretation of
western man's economic drive as sublimated anal eroticism has been notably discussed by Norman O. Brown in his chapter "Filthy Lucre," *Life Against Death* (New
York, 1959).

[10]Both Paul's family situation and his league with sinister forces bear an interesting resemblance also to the story of Hamlet, which Freud discusses in "The 'Uncanny,' " *Collected Papers*, LV, p. 382. Like Oedipus (and Lawrence's Paul), Hamlet
is the typically introverted and incestuous hero of "the family romance," whose
frustrated sexual desires lead to fantasies about ghosts and he development of acute
intellectual and prophetic powers.

discusses in this regard, elements of the sexually perverse become instrumental in Paul's primitive invocation of the daemonic agencies who bring foreknowledge and incredible fortune before destroying their petitioners. In "From The Neurosis of Demoniacal Possession in The Seventeenth Century" Freud delves into an analysis of the Faustus type with regard to the case history of one Christolph Haitzmann, an impecunious painter who formed an imaginary pact with the devil in his maddened struggle for success:

> All he wanted was security in life, at first with the help of Satan but at the cost of eternal bliss. . . . Perhaps Christolph Haitzmann was only a poor devil, one of those who never had any luck; perhaps he was too poorly gifted, too ineffective to make a living, and belonged to that well known type, 'the eternal suckling'—to those who are unable to tear themselves away from . . . the mother's breast, who hold fast all their lives to their claim to be nourished by someone else. And so in his illness our painter followed the path from his own father by way of the Devil as father-substitute. . . . (IV, 470-71)

Juxtapose Freud's summary of Haitzmann with Uncle Oscar's wry /387/ eulogy for Paul: "My God Hester, you're eighty odd thousand to the good, and a poor devil of a son to the bad. But poor devil, poor devil, he's best gone out of a life where he rides his rocking-horse to find a winner." Both Haitzmann and Paul share a belief in an essentially daemonic capitalism which magically gives something for nothing, but in the end claims all. We might also compare the regressive tendencies of Freud's Faustus type with the symbolic fate of Clifford Chatterley, the paradigmatic capitalist who ends rooting at the breast of Mrs. Bolton. While several critics have mentioned Lawrence's use of the traditional association of hobbyhorses with witchcraft and the occult,[11] Freud provides us with a full and specific understanding of Paul's demonism. Lawrence, too, was likely to have been interested in Freud's essays dealing with witchcraft, the uncanny, and the occult, since they more or less confirm his own psychological reading of *The Scarlet Letter*. It is the name of Paul's mother, Hester Cresswell, which suggests our next line of investigation into Lawrence's obscure suggestions of sorcery and witchcraft.

In Lawrence's notorious essay on *The Scarlet Letter* we find close and illuminating analogies with Paul's crucial relationship with his parents. Lawrence's imaginative reading of Hawthorne's romance

---

[11]I refer to the appended commentaries of Robert Gorham Davis in *Ten Modern Masters* (New York, 1959) and Gordon and Tate in *The House of Fiction* (New York 1950).

depends mainly on an interpretation of Dimmesdale and Hester Prynne as Americanized types of Adam and Eve. Hester's seduction of the minister is supposedly motivated by her feminine desire for revenge (largely a product of sexual frustration, it would appear) against the authority of the New England patriarchate which he embodies. Hester Prynne's psycho-sexual motivation, at least in Lawrence's interpretation, thus corresponds with that of Hester Cresswell in "The Rocking-Horse Winner." We have also discovered a possible attempt at historical allegory in Lawrence's story, insofar as Paul seems to parody various heroic and tragic types of Western man. Lawrence reads *The Scarlet Letter* as an historical allegory of the fall of Puritan New England and the rise of an effeminate neo-Aztec culture in America. His revisions of the Hawthorne essay, as Armin Arnold's edition of the uncollected versions has shown, harp on this "prophetic" meaning, greatly distorting Hawthorne's book in the interests of a Lawrentian jeremiad against the American twentieth century. Hester's child Pearl (the symbol of Eastern luxury) completes her mother's demonic rebellion against the Puritan state with the brilliant tactic of marrying an Italian nobleman (a display /388/ of fondness for the Mediterranean male to be generally noted in Lawrence's later heroines).[12] Lawrence is more than Miltonic in ascribing to Hester an uncontrollable and destructive sensuousness, and gains substantial support from Hawthorne's own descriptions of her "rich, voluptuous oriental characteristic," and "taste for the gorgeously beautiful." Cruelly denied by the Puritan ethic, Hester's suppressed desire for "luxury" (like "luck" an ambiguous term with sexual connotations) issues in an unconsciously spiteful revenge against the social order, a subversion Lawrence cheerfully identifies with witchcraft. "The ancients," he writes, "were not altogether fools in their belief in witchcraft. When the profound subconscious soul of woman recoils from its creative union with man it can exact a tremendous invisible destructive force."[13]

Lawrence's description of the relationship between Hester and Pearl makes an interesting gloss on the analogous situation between Hester Cresswell and Paul, and bears directly on the themes of witchcraft and infanticide in Lawrence's story. What Lawrence calls Hester

---

[12]The demonic mother and daughter combination appearing in *St. Mawr* and in the short story "Mother and Daughter" are prefigured by Christiana and Diana Crich in *Women in Love*, who represent demonized versions of Mrs. Morel and Miriam of the earlier *Sons and Lovers*.

[13]D. H. Lawrence, *The Symbolic Meaning. The Uncollected Versions of Studies in Classic American Literature*, edited by Armin Arnold with a preface by Harry T. Moore (Fontwell, Arundel, 1961), p. 146.

Prynne's "Astarte" or "Hecate" principle "has in it a necessary antagonism to life itself, the very issue of life: it contains in it the element of blood sacrifice of children, in its darker, destructive mood."[14] In "The Rocking-Horse Winner," Hester Cresswell's sexual disappointment results in a similarly inordinate and destructive craving for substitute "luxuries," and in a like resentment of her child. According to Lawrence, Hester Prynne "simply *hates* her child, from one part of herself. And from another, she cherishes her child as her own precious treasure. For Pearl is the continuing of her female revenge on life. But female revenge hits both ways. Hits back at its own mother."[15] Hester Cresswell, too, resents her children as being "thrust upon her." At the story's conclusion, however, "all her tormented motherhood flooding upon her," she rushes to the prostrate form of the son she has destroyed.

The major difference between the plot situations of Hawthorne's romance and "The Rocking-Horse Winner" is that Lawrence has neatly substituted Freud's Oedipal boy for both Hester's lover Dimmesdale and little Pearl in order to strengthen his tragic-comic /389/ fable. At one dramatic stroke Hester Cresswell is bereft of both child and lover, all save the 80,000 pounds which now ironically fail to comfort her. In the Hawthorne essays Lawrence interprets Dimmesdale as an Oedipal male destroyed by the stronger feminine will of an Astarte or Magna Mater, a female archetype which in Jungian terminology "takes possession" of Hester's soul and turns her into a "witch." It is in this same psychological sense that we are meant to accept the uncanny goings on in the Cresswell's haunted house, a matriarchal institution presided over not by the father but by the maternal uncle. Quite simply, the theme of "The Rocking-Horse Winner" (as of Lawrence's equally satirical "Mother and Daughter") is that matriarchy is the devil—man's just punishment for failing to assert his phallic divinity. A further and very important parallel exists between the spiritual narcissism of Arthur Dimmesdale and that of young Paul which further indicates the range of Lawrence's riding metaphor. Here is the Lawrentian version of Hawthorne's hero:

> Mr. Dimmesdale . . . had lived by governing his body, ruling it in the interests of his spirit. Now he has a good time all by himself torturing his body, whipping it, piercing it with thorns, macerating himself. It's a form of masturbation. He wants to get

[14]*The Symbolic Meaning*, p. 147.

[15]D. H. Lawrence, *Studies in Classic American Literature* (New York, 1953), p. 108.

a mental grip on his body. And since he can't quite manage it with the mind, witness his fall—he will give it what for, with whips. His will shall *lash* his body.... It is the old self mutilation gone rotten.[16]

As we have noted, Freud's work with "uncanny" children gives a psychological interpretation of demonic offspring such as Hawthorne's Pearl which undoubtedly would have interested Lawrence. There is little difficulty in seeing Freud's ideas at work, for example, in this analysis of Hester's daughter: "And Pearl, by the very openness of her perversity, was more straightforward than her parents. She flatly refused any Heavenly Father, seeing the earthly one such a fraud."[17] Thus the discrediting of the real father both in Lawrence's version of *The Scarlet Letter* and in "The Rocking-Horse Winner" precipitates the tragedy. And, as we have seen, this pattern conforms with the Freudian analysis of the Faust figure. Hester dresses Pearl as the tiny image of the luxury she denies herself, just as Paul becomes his mother's idea of the lucky lover, and ideal replacement for her dismal husband. When Hester asks Paul how he knows he is "lucky," he brazenly declares, "God told me"—a blasphemous indication of his sinister league with the Dark Father. This deity, it would appear, is the God of the Witches, the "father substitute" erected in the un-/390/ conscious of the Oedipal child as a maneuver against the God of his Fathers.

Our last concern remains with Lawrence's finely controlled use of the fantastic and the uncanny in this story, which bears a strong resemblance to Kafka's tragi-comedies "The Metamorphosis" and "The Judgment"—fables which also depend on our accepting the external reality of an Oedipal regression fantasy. It may be pointed out here that it was Freud's recommended practice to suspend, for the purpose of analysis, the rational distinction between fact and fantasy in his patients' autobiographical narratives. With this apparently unscientific attitude Freud found that he arrived more quickly at the essence of the problem. His method of analysis thus corresponds interestingly with Hawthorne's quest for a "romantic precinct" in which the writer could demonstrate the "truth of the heart." "In contrast to *material* reality," Freud asserts, "these phantasies possess *psychical* reality, and we gradually come to understand that in the world of neurosis PSYCHICAL REALITY *is the determining factor.*"[18]

---

[16]*Studies in Classic American Literature*, p. 100.

[17]*Studies in Classic American Literature*, p. 108.

[18]*A General Introduction To Psychoanalysis*, p. 378. Caps and italics Freud's.

"The Rocking-Horse Winner," like Kafka's "Metamorphosis" and Hawthorne's "Wakefield," for example, persuades us to accept the universal reality of a personal nightmare. Lawrence's profound difference from these writers lies in his relatively cheerful attitude toward the inescapable irrationality of human nature. Where Kafka finds submission to the irrational forces of the unconscious a personal tragedy implying the permanent destruction of self, Lawrence sees the surrender of the ego as the condition of rebirth. Whereas Freud's goal is the defense and aggrandisement of the old ego, Lawrence's purpose is the renewal of our emotional and communal life. In this respect Lawrence's thinking resembles the theories of Jung and those of such socially oriented American psychologists as Lawrence's late correspondent, Trigant Burrow.

Like other "schismatics," however, Lawrence shared more fundamental assumptions with Freud, including ideas about literature, than their differences would indicate. In his essay on the uncanny, which stresses its effective literary uses, Freud tells us that the creator of the uncanny tale ". . . has a peculiarly directive influence over us; by means of the states of mind into which he can put us and the expectations he can rouse in us, he is able to guide the current of our emotions, dam it up in one direction and make it flow in another . . ." (IV, 406). In obvious reference to his own work, Lawrence writes in the famous authorial intrusion in Chapter IX of *Lady Chatterley's* /391/ *Lover:* "For even satire is a form of sympathy. It is the way our sympathy flows and recoils that really determines our lives. And here is the vast importance of the novel, properly handled. It can inform and lead into new places the flow of our sympathetic consciousness, and it can lead our sympathy away in recoil from things gone dead." As satire, "The Rocking-Horse Winner" is intended to make us feel emotional as well as intellectual revulsion from the inorganic death-in-life of the middle class menage and, accordingly, a greater respect for the traditional view of a family unified under the vital authority of the father. For Lawrence the "phallic" family unit was the microcosmic model of the healthy world state. Paul's frenzied rocking satirizes the insanity of existence in a mechanically organized environment as opposed to real living as Lawrence describes it in *Apocalypse*, where he admonishes: "What we want is to destroy our false, inorganic connections, especially those related to money, and reestablish the living organic connections with the cosmos, the sun and earth, with mankind and nation and family."[19] Paul's precocious search for

---

[19] D. H. Lawrence, *Apocalypse* (New York, 1936), p. 200.

intellectual certainty or "knowledge" about the external universe, as
Lawrence explains in *Fantasia of The Unconscious*, should have been
hastily discouraged: "A child mustn't understand things. He must
have his own way. His vision isn't ours. When a boy of eight sees a
horse, he doesn't see the correct biological object we intend him to
see. He sees a big living presence of no particular shape with hair
dangling from its neck and four legs."[20]

The symbolic meaning of Paul's rocking-horse depends precisely
on the fact that it is not "a big living presence," but an artificial
object. When his mother remonstrates, "Surely you're too big for a
rocking-horse!" Paul cryptically explains, "Well, you see, Mother, till
I can have a *real* horse, I like to have *some* sort of animal about."
Modern man, Lawrence thus implies, has lost the real, living universe
which is still present to the unreflective child and the savage. Lawrence's advocacy of a return to a primitive epistemology links him
less with Freud, of course, than with Jung and with the whole development of Romantic theories of cognition from Blake and Coleridge
to the present. Allied to Paul's precocity and symptomatic of his over-
developed intellectuality is the boy's narcissism. Like the Morel
brothers and Gerald Crich, Paul is the type of Oedipal introvert
Lawrence deplores as a characteristically modern child in the chapter
"Parent Love" in *Fantasia of The Unconscious:* "And today /392/
what have we but this? Almost inevitably we find in a child now an
intense, precocious, secret sexual preoccupation. The upper self is
rabidly engaged in exploiting the lower self. A child and its own
roused, inflamed sex, its own shame and masturbation, its own cruel,
secret sexual excitement and sex *curiosity*, this is the greatest tragedy
of our day."[21] And it is this tragedy which Lawrence epitomizes in
Paul's fall from his hobbyhorse.

The image of the equestrian, used as an emblem of modern man's
tragic attempt at conscious domination of his libido, is a recurrent
figure in Lawrence's fiction, appearing in *Women in Love*, "The Prussian Officer," and most of the New Mexico stories. In *Lady Chatterley's Lover* this image undergoes minor but significant variation.
Clifford, whose instinctive life is completely moribund, is placed in
a motorized wheelchair. Where *Lady Chatterley* and the later novels
generally fail to mediate between Lawrence's subjective view of the
modern condition and the public reality, his shorter fiction very
often succeeds. "There is, in fact, a path from phantasy back again

---

[20]D. H. Lawrence, *Psychoanalysis and The Unconscious/Fantasia of The Unconscious* (New York, 1960), pp. 125-26.
[21]*Psychoanalysis and The Unconscious ...*, p. 155.

to reality," Freud acknowledges, "—and that is art."[22] Lawrence's novels too frequently point out that there is another path that leads from reality to fantasy—and that is self-expression. In "The Rocking-Horse Winner" Lawrence reveals an ability to create this artistic mid-realm granted to few writers, and then, as Hawthorne sadly realized, only occasionally.

[22]*A General Introduction To Psychoanalysis,* p. 384.

Frank Amon

D. H. Lawrence
and the Short Story*

I

The controversies over the position of D. H. Lawrence as major apostle, prophet, or pathological study have almost run their course. Lawrence has had his winter sleep. Now almost for the first time since his death in 1930, interest has begun consciously to center on his status as a literary artist, a status acutely in need of a fresh critical examination.

Such an examination might well begin with Lawrence's short stories. More concentrated but less complex than his novels, they introduce many of the nuclear symbols, patterns, and themes essential to all his art. Yet an author's short stories, as Elizabeth Bowen has rightly said, stand to be judged first on their merits *as* stories, and only later in their relation to his other works.

It is my contention that Lawrence's stories, regardless of their relation to his novels, disclose an original and significant release of his faculties and that they stand as a special and unique achievement in the art of the short story. I intend to illustrate this through an examination of three of Lawrence's stories: "The Odour of Chrysanthemums," "The Prussian Officer," and "The Rocking-Horse Winner." They are not, I think, superior—with the possible exception of "The Prussian Officer"—to some dozen other of his stories. But they will serve to illustrate my point, and I have particular reasons, which will be considered later, for choosing them.

Lawrence, like Chekhov, stands for a distension in the form /223/

*Reprinted from *The Achievement of D. H. Lawrence,* eds. Frederick J. Hoffman and Harry T. Moore (Norman: University of Oklahoma Press, 1953), pp. 222-234, by permission. Copyright 1953 by the University of Oklahoma Press.

of the story. Like Chekhov, he had the genius for portraying the intimate feeling of a place, a landscape, a conversation, or a character. Like Chekhov—but in a manner peculiar to his technique—he crystallized vacancy, frustration, inertia, and futile aspiration. We see that all of Lawrence's stories share one characteristic: all depend, as stories, upon subtle psychological changes of character.

With Lawrence's characters (as with Chekhov's) the subconscious seems to come to the surface and they communicate directly without the impediment of speech. Naturally the most interesting point for Lawrence is that at which the interplay of psychic forces is incomplete, where the adjustment is difficult, where the emphasis is on discord rather than on harmony. Consequently, Lawrence focused his attention, as Frederick Hoffman has said, "on the subtle complexity of an emotional state which a character assumes in a crisis."

The significance of this is that Lawrence has accomplished a transfiguration of experience. He lifts his characters from the surface experience of the concrete world onto new and immediate levels of psychic consciousness, and then returns them, sanctified and altered, to the concrete world in which they must continue. Inevitably this is the symbolic *rites de passage*, the ceremony or initiation or baptism, which ushers an individual into a new way of life; and in this, too, it is the spiritual death and rebirth motif of Lawrence's chosen symbol, the Phoenix.

II

If we take, for example, "The Odour of Chrysanthemums," one of Lawrence's earliest stories, written in 1909, this *rites de passage* aspect comes out quite clearly.

The autobiographical setting of Lawrence's youth—the lower-class colliery family—is of course common to many of his early stories and novels. But the theme, too, is central to Lawrence: the inviolable isolation of the individual psyche, the utter separateness of those with whom we share physical intimacy.

The revelation of the theme (of which for us the entire story is the qualifying and modifying symbol) comes to the wife through /224/ the death of her husband. Revelation through death then is the means of objectifying the theme. However, it is the *moment* of revelation with which we are concerned here and with the peculiar means of objectifying that moment.

Gradually, as the story unfolds, our interest in the chrysanthemums increases. At first, they hang dishevelled, "like pink cloths." A little later, Elizabeth's small son tears at the "ragged wisps of chrysanthemums" and drops the petals in handfuls along the path: " 'Don't do that—it does look nasty,' said his mother. He refrained, and she, suddenly pitiful, broke off a twig with three or four wan flowers and held them against her face." When they reach the yard, she hesitates and instead of laying the flowers aside, she pushes them in her apron band. Later, when the family has had tea and the father has not returned, Elizabeth's daughter wants to smell the flowers:

> "Don't they smell beautiful!"
> Her mother gave a short laugh.
> "No," she said, "not to me. It was chrysanthemums when I married him, and chrysanthemums when you were born, and the first time they ever brought him home drunk, he'd got brown chrysanthemums in his button-hole."

Here then is their significance: they are talismans of change, transition into a new way of life—a tragic way of life. They are markers of marriage, birth, and—inevitably—death. The chrysanthemums, we might say, are the omens, and it is through them that a great part of our interest is aroused and focalized; and it is through them (but not through them alone) that the father's death is foreshadowed.

There is, however, a more subtle change than the physical death of the father. The dead man is brought in and laid out on the parlor floor. The wife and the husband's mother are present. The room is dimly lit by a single candle in a lustre-glass. Two vases of chrysanthemums exude a cold, deathly smell. Together the wife and mother strip the man naked and kneel on opposite sides to wash him of the pit grime: /225/

> They worked thus in silence for a long time. They never forgot it was death, and the touch of the man's dead body gave them strange emotions, different in each of the women; a great dread possessed them both, the mother felt the lie was given to her womb, she was denied; the wife felt the utter isolation of the human soul, the child within her was a weight apart from her.
> At last it was finished. He was a man of handsome body, and his face showed no traces of drink. He was blond, full-fleshed, with fine limbs. But he was dead.

Few readers will miss in this scene the obvious relation to a ceremonial preparation of the dead. For this ritual purification and consecration rite performed by the nearest kin has an archetypal significance. More specifically it resembles the ritual consecration

of the archetypal parent, the father as the sacrificial King, the Fallen
and Forsaken God.

It is significant, however, that Lawrence has chosen this symbolic
enactment as the appropriate action to objectify the moment of inner
revelation which comes across, it would seem, out of death; for as
Elizabeth washes the dead body, she realizes the impregnable separateness of this man with whom she has been living as one flesh: "She
had said he was something he was not; she had felt familiar with him.
Whereas he was apart all the while, living as she never lived, feeling
as she never felt." And she is "grateful to death, which restored the
truth." It is the reversal of Donne's "No man is an island, entire of
itself" to "*Each* man is an island, never fully known," a revelation
through death of a mystery of life; and the living, as well as the dead,
has undergone a transition: "She saw this episode of her life closed."
"Then with peace sunk heavy on her heart, she went about making
tidy the kitchen."

Lawrence wrote this story when he was twenty-four; but he revised
it five years later. We need not concern ourselves with the fact that
Lawrence was reading Jane Harrison's *Ancient Art and Ritual* about
the same time he was making his revision. What is important is that
he could thoroughly incorporate into his art the most /226/ appropriate action—literal and symbolic—to objectify his theme.

We find incipient in this story such other patterns and motifs as the
Mater Dolorata, possessive motherhood, lack of rapport between the
sexes, and father-hatred-envy, which were to occupy Lawrence the
rest of his life.

Lawrence developed rapidly as a writer, and his quickening command of form and subject matter is evident in his first six years of
production. By the time he was twenty-five he had written one of the
world's masterpieces of short fiction, "The Prussian Officer." Lawrence
recognized its worth in a letter to Edward Garnett at the time: "I
have written the best story I have ever done—about a German officer
in the army and his orderly." It is this of course—and much more.

For the pattern of the Handsome Soldier and his tragic death has a
mythic counterpart.[1] It suggests that universal motif, the fable of the
Fall of Man, the loss of Paradise. For the orderly is, on one level at
least, Primal Man. Indeed, it is said of him that he seemed "never to
have thought, only to have received life direct through his senses, and
acted straight from instinct." He has a sweetheart, "a girl from the

---

[1]A remarkable parallel of theme and treatment of theme is found in Herman
Melville's *Billy Budd*.

mountains, independent and primitive. . . . He went with her not to
talk, but to have his arm around her, and for the physical contact. . . .
And she, in some unspoken fashion, was there for him. They loved
each other."

If the orderly is the Adam of this Eden, the Captain is its Satan.
Maleficent as he is, the Captain, like the arch-fiend in *Paradise Lost,*
has a certain nobility of stature, an aura of the Fallen Prince about
him ("He had ruined his prospects in the Army, and remained an
infantry captain.") :

> The Captain was a tall man of about forty, grey at the temples.
> He had a handsome, finely knit figure and was one of the best
> horsemen in the West. . . . Perhaps the man was the more hand-
> some for the deep lines in his face, the irritable tension of his
> brow, which gave him the look of a man who fights with life.
> His fair eyebrows stood bushy over light blue eyes that were
> always flashing fire. /227/

An Aryan Mephistopheles, he is the perfect prototype of the Prussian
Kriegsadel. In contrast to his orderly, he is a man completely "dominated by mind," a man of "passionate temper who had always kept
himself suppressed." He had never married, for his position did not
allow it, and "no woman had ever moved him to it." "Whereas the
young soldier seemed to live out his warm, full nature, to give it off
in his very movements, which had a certain zest, such as wild animals
have in free movement." And it is precisely this guileless nature that
the Captain hates and tempts to action.

The Captain's predisposition to iniquity is innate in him, however,
not the product of training or intellect but a trait hitherto repressed.
It takes the form of an instinctive hatred for innocence and good, but
a hatred so obsessive and even paranoid as to suggest the perversion
of a still more deep-rooted love.

And if there are mythic overtones of the Biblical temptation and
fall (the youth's limitations as a human being lead him to commit in
fact a capital crime), there are also psychological undertones of
homosexuality. For it is in effect the story of a courtship. From the
first, the orderly feels that he is "connected" with the figure of the
Captain — "and damned by it." While rubbing his Captain down, he
admires the "amazing riding muscles of his loins." Once, when a
bottle of wine had gone over, the Captain's eyes, "bluey like fire," had
held the youth: "It was a shock for the young soldier. He felt something sink deeper, deeper into his soul, where nothing had ever gone
before. It left him rather blank and wondering. Some of his natural

completeness in himself was gone, a little uneasiness took its place. And from that time an undiscovered feeling had held between the two men."

As for the Captain, he had "become aware of his servant's young, vigorous, unconscious presence about him." And it was like a "warm flame upon the older man's tense, rigid body." He is attracted to the youth's "strong young shoulders" and "the bend of his neck." We have the feeling throughout the story of a homosexual courtship: the older man, in spite of himself, wooing the younger; and the youth, sensing the advances, repudiating the Captain.

And with the soldier's denial, it becomes more difficult for /228/ the Captain to restrain himself: "As yet, the soldier had held himself off from the elder man. The Captain grew madly irritable. He could not rest when the soldier was away, and when he was present, he glared at him with tormented eyes. . . . he was infuriated by the free movement of the handsome limbs. . . . And he became harsh and cruelly bullying. . . ." And it would seem impossible to ignore this homosexual aspect in such a statement as "The officer tried hard not to admit the passion that had got hold of him. He would not know that his feeling for his orderly was anything but that of a man incensed by his stupid, perverse servant. So, keeping quite justified and conventional in his consciousness, he let the other thing run on."

Finally, the officer's passion culminates in an outburst of rage when the soldier in confusion ignores a question. As the orderly is crouching to set down a load of dishes before a stairway, the captain kicks him, sending the dishes tumbling; and as the soldier clings to the bannister pillar for support, the captain kicks him repeatedly. And afterwards, when the orderly confesses that he had been writing some poetry:

"Poetry, what poetry?" asked the Captain, with a sickly smile.
Again there was the working in the throat. The Captain's heart had suddenly gone down heavily, and he stood sick and tired.
"For my girl, sir," he heard the dry, inhuman sound.
"Oh!" he said, turning away. "Clear the table."

Here, on one level, is the Captain's realization that he can never succeed. The sinking of his heart and the curt dismissal of the orderly would seem to indicate his acknowledgement of a rival and the futility of the pursuit. In fact he erases the incident from his mind, denies it to himself — and is "successful in his denial."

With the soldier it is a different matter. He feels that he has been violated emotionally and physically, and he is filled with "one single, sleep-heavy intention: to save himself." The maneuvers are the following morning; and the combination of his bruises, the marching, the hot sun, and the violation of his inner self /229/ moves him — when he and the officer are alone — to attack the Captain and choke him to death. And it is only through this act of purgation that he is temporarily restored: "pressing with all his heart behind in a passion of relief, the tension of his wrists exquisite with relief."

In one sense, this is a victory — a victory over and a release from the evil dominance of the Captain. But, in another sense, it is a capitulation, for this is what the orderly has been continuously fighting against. It is foreshadowed earlier in the story with the statement that "in spite of himself the hate grew, responsive to the officer's passion." And it is for this surrender to the Captain, as well as for the criminal act, that the orderly pays with his life.

I have postponed until now a consideration of the nature imagery in this story. For although it is intimately related to — and is in fact a part of — both the mythic and sexual patterns, it serves a wider and, if possible, more profound purpose. I refer specifically to the emotional significance of the valley-garden-mountain imagery which is wrought into the pattern of the story. At the beginning of the story the soldiers are marching along a white, hot road:

> On either hand, the valley, wide and shallow, glittered with heat; dark green patches of rye, pale young corn, fallow and meadow and black pine woods spread in a dull, hot diagram under a glistening sky. But right in front the mountains ranged across, pale blue and very still, snow gleaming gently out of the deep atmosphere. And towards the mountains, on and on, the regiment marched between the rye fields and the meadows, between the scraggy fruit trees set regularly on either side of the high road. The burnished, dark green rye threw off a suffocating heat, the mountains drew gradually nearer and more distinct. . . .
>
> He [the orderly] walked on and on in silence, staring at the mountains ahead, that rose sheer out of the land, and stood fold behind fold, half earth, half heaven, the barrier with slits of soft snow, in the pale, bluish peaks.

We perceive in terms of spatial contrasts the life of the body, down /230/ in the hot suffocating valley, challenged by the allurement of mountain heights. The contending opposites communicate a distinctive sense of the life of the earth in tension with the heaven of the spirit. The flux and heat of the soldier's sensuous experience — intoxicating and soporific — becomes at once a challenge and a bondage: a challenge because of the strange allurement of the mountain snows and a bondage or crucifixion because he cannot escape — or can escape only through death.

This theme — the conflict of the flesh and the spirit — is of course common to many of Lawrence's works, and the valley-mountain cluster with the same connotations can be found in such of his novels as *Women in Love* and *The Lost Girl,* in the poem "Meeting in the Mountains," and in the first pages of his travel essays (with a valuable commentary), *Twilight in Italy.*

In the story the theme becomes more and more explicit after the fateful beating. The orderly feels that the snowy peaks, radiant in the sky, and the "whity-green glacier river," in the valley below, seem almost supernatural, but at the same time he is going mad with fever and thirst. And near the end of the story, when he is in a delirium of fever, he sees "the mountains in a wonderlight, not far away and radiant. Behind the soft, grey ridge of the nearest range the further mountains stood golden and pale grey, the snow all radiant like pure, soft gold. . . . And like the golden, lustrous gleaming of the snow he felt his own thirst bright in him. And everything slid away." He remains in a state of delirium throughout the night, but in the morning, straight in front of him are the mountains: "He wanted them — he wanted them alone — he wanted to leave himself and be identified with them." And he does attain his realization — through death:

> There they ranked, all still and wonderful between earth and heaven. He stared till his eyes went black, and the mountains, as they stood in their beauty, so clean and cool, seemed to have it, that which was lost in him.

No one would suppose that the mythic, the psychological, and the image function separately, alternating perhaps from one level to the other like the negative and positive charges in a flow of /231/ electric current. One in fact *is* the other, and all operate more or less simultaneously while we follow the literal level. And we must never forget that the literal is there, for if it is not there, we have no story. It is important to note, however, that, regardless of levels of meaning, the distinctive characteristic is the flow and conflict of *opposites:* officer-soldier, aristocrat-peasant, evil-innocence, homosexual-heterosexual, mind-instinct, flesh-spirit, valley-mountain; and Freudians would see a father-son dichotomy.

No one would suppose either that the complex of these three levels of meaning is *equivalent* to the story itself. In fact, I have ignored the social and political implications: the way in which the malady of the individual psyche can become the malady of modern civilization, the prostitution of the instincts by the perverted mechanized forces of the over-intellectualized world.

For the malady of the individual psyche reflecting the malady of modern civilization assumes various patterns in Lawrence's art. Paul, in *Sons and Lovers,* and Gerald, in *Women in Love,* depict different aspects of this theme. And in the story of Paul in "The Rocking-Horse Winner" Lawrence has adapted an age-old form to his subject matter.

"The Rocking-Horse Winner" is the story of Paul who secretly rides his rocking horse to pick winners in the horse races. Paul manages to win ten thousand pounds, five thousand of which he gives anonymously to his mother because she is "unlucky" and because the house whispers: *There must be more money!* His powers fail, however, and Paul becomes desperate and wild-eyed as the day for the big Derby draws near and he still does not know the winner. Finally, in the middle of the night, his mother finds him in a trance-like state furiously riding his rocking horse: "It's Malabar!" he screams. "It's Malabar!" and collapses in a brain fever. Paul is deliriously ill for three days, but on the third he learns that his horse has won, and he dies in the night, knowing that he *is* lucky. The tale ends with his uncle telling Paul's mother: "He's best gone out of a life where he rides his rocking-horse to find a winner!"

The allegorical implications of "The Rocking-Horse Winner" would seem evident in this last speech. More specifically, however, it has several characteristics common to the form of the /232/ fable or Märchen of folklore. Like the fable, it has two parts: the narrative which exemplifies a moral, and the statement of the moral appended in the form of proverb. Moreover, the syntactical and rhetorical devices of the opening paragraph — "There was a woman who was beautiful, yet she had no luck. She married for love, and the love turned to dust." — exploit a formulaic beginning common to most Märchen, the characters not named, and some explanation concerning the cause of the difficulty which the story is to illustrate dramatically ("A King had a daughter who was beautiful beyond all measure, but so proud and haughty withal..."). And in fact the whispering house and the powers of divination ascribed to Paul (an ironic variation of the Rags-to-Riches motif through the supernatural powers of the first-born son) indicate to what extent Lawrence went to establish the tone and atmosphere of a modern moral fable.

The theme of the story is implied in the moral proverb that Lawrence invented: Don't ride your rocking horse to find a winner. The story illustrates the point. The mother realizes that she is unlucky, but she does not recognize the true reason as stated in the first paragraph: "At the center of her heart was a hard little place that could not feel love, no, not for anybody." She realizes that she is incapable of loving and that she is unlucky, but she does not equate the two in terms of cause and effect.

Instead she rationalizes the problem and tells Paul that they are the "poor members of the family" because his father has no luck. For she makes the common mistake of equating luck with money. Thus she tells Paul that luck is "what causes you to have money." Consequently, Paul is the victim, in a sense, of his mother's reasoning (a common pattern among Lawrence's heroes, with the subsidiary pattern of the father as scapegoat).

In reality, the family is not poor. They have a fine house and garden, servants and gardener; and the mother, as well as the father, has a small independent income. The fact is that each of them has expensive tastes and indulges them, for in spite of the shortage of money, "the style was always kept up."

The whole family is, in Lawrence's metaphor, riding its rocking horse to find a winner, riding furiously and fanatically and getting nowhere. /233/

One also sees elements of the ritual dance in Paul's rocking-horse episodes. Lawrence of course knew the English morris and the Abbots Bromley Antler dance, both of which have hobby-horse riders. But more than likely he was remembering the famous hobby dance of Padstow, Cornwall or the New Mexican pueblos' saints' impersonations, called *maiyanyi*. But whatever Lawrence's source, his choice was a happy one. For the ritual riding of a hobbyhorse has a primordial depth and scope that extends into antiquity and throughout disparate cultures. In the Balinese *sanghang djanar*, for example, the rider — like Paul — rides in a trancelike state.

More fundamentally, the rocking horse (a "false" horse) is the perfect symbol to embody humanity's trancelike and mechanistic plunging onward to nowhere. Moreover, the choice of the rocking horse as the divining medium is psychologically sound. Divination is a form of sympathetic magic in which the *status* of the divining medium determines the future event. Both the indicator and the event are in a relation of logical harmony. And it is signifiicant that the event divined, the horse race itself, is as appropriate a symbol as the rocking horse for mankind's materialistic and competitive race back to its point of departure.

III

This consideration of the three stories—"Odour of Chrysanthemums," "The Prussian Officer," and "The Rocking-Horse Winner" — should confirm my point: that Lawrence has a special and unique contribution to offer in the art of the short story. I have not considered to any extent Lawrence's prose style, which serves its subject consummately. Rather I have dealt with his subject, the discovery under the social surface of more opulent realms of being.

For the effect of D. H. Lawrence's art, and it is also its value, is that it gives a new meaning to our experience. Lawrence's command of life, significant life, was such that we discover in his fiction a new content — an immediacy and relevance that was not previously perceived. An emotion with Lawrence is an apotheosis. Through its elemental and seminal processes of action it is a /234/ transition into another sphere of being, a *rite de passage*. And once having experienced this, a character is never quite the same: Elizabeth, after the washing-purification; the orderly, after the choking-purgation; and Paul, after the riding-divination. Lawrence has captured this moment of transition, reinforced it with an emotionally charged symbol (chrysanthemums, valley-garden-mountain, rocking horse-horse race), and perpetuated it on the printed page.

Lawrence commanded his art so completely as to suggest less discipline than it had. There is in him an uninterrupted communication between his thought and his senses. This deceptive ease of style has contributed to a myth concerning his method of composition: that he preferred not — as most authors do when dissatisfied with what they have written — to file, clip, insert, and transpose (see Aldous Huxley's Introduction to the *Letters*, p. xvii), but rather to rewrite entire new drafts straight off the pen in new bursts of spontaneity and intuition.

This assumption in itself is unimportant, for it is not the author's creative processes but the work itself which is evaluated. This method attributed to Lawrence, however, has served several critics as a point of departure in attacking his "looseness" and "diffuseness." No doubt — like all great artists — Lawrence's first conception of an idea was involuntary, a "vital fortuity"; and perhaps his *first* drafts were written in bursts of spontaneity. But his revisions were certainly voluntary and meticulous.

My interpretations would argue that few artists could be more consciously and pertinently preoccupied with problems of method, technique, and form.

Frederick W. Turner, III

Prancing in to a Purpose: Myths, Horses, and True Selfhood in Lawrence's "The Rocking-Horse Winner"*

What ails me is the absolute frustration of my primeval societal instinct. The hero illusion starts with the individualist illusion, and all other resistances ensue. I think societal instinct much deeper than sex instinct — and societal repression much more devastating. There is no repression of the sexual individual comparable to the repression of the societal man in me, by the individual ego, my own and everybody else's. I am weary even of my own individuality, and simply nauseated by other people's.[1]

So wrote D. H. Lawrence to Dr. Trigant Burrow in the summer of 1927. For a man in Lawrence's condition the sentiments expressed in the letter are hardly surprising: his health continued to fail, and he must have known that he was dying. As the shadows lengthen on the lawn it is natural for a man to be sensibly impressed with human limitations, his own and everybody else's, to be almost unutterably aware of the terrifying narrowness of the individual self and of the human self. So it was with Lawrence, and as one reads through the letters, the literature, and the posthumous papers of the last years one sees that these realizations gnawed at the writer as persistently as his incurable disease.[2]

Beyond the specifically physical genesis of such a concern there was in Lawrence's case an emotional reason as well. The history of his

---

*This article was written especially for this volume. Quotations and paraphrases from the article can be documented by citing the page numbers of this casebook.

[1]In Diana Trilling (ed.), *Selected Letters of D. H. Lawrence* (New York, 1961), p. 288.

[2]Mary Freeman's study of Lawrence's ideas, *D. H. Lawrence* (New York, 1955), contains several excellent passages discussing this driving concern.

emotional career is that of a long series of painful, tangled, enervating relationships with all sorts of people in all sorts of places. Lawrence could not help involving himself deeply in the lives of those with whom he came in contact because he was a generous man; but he also deplored the results of such entanglements — the misunderstandings, the bruises, and above all, the inevitable warring of separate egos. So in these last years with his own fires burning hotter even as they dwindled, he carried on a kind of love-hate relationship with his friends.

And then there were occupational reasons too for Lawrence's consuming desire to somehow move beyond ego-centrism, for the artist is a man devoted to the expression of self through the exercise of the imagination. Few writers in the modern era have been more aware of themselves as artists, aware of the peculiar cultural and psychological problems of the artist's life, than Lawrence was. Henry James had a similarly acute sense of himself as an artist, and he left a long string of novels and tales which may be read as fictional workings out of his own situation. In fact, one of these, "The Pupil," bears a striking similarity to "The Rocking-Horse Winner" which it is the purpose of this essay to discuss. Both James and Lawrence were troubled by the artist's inevitable expression of self, of ego, in his work. Both were aware, as Aldous Huxley wrote of Lawrence, that the artist's "gift is his fate, and he follows a predestined course from which no ordinary power can deflect him."[3] Moreover, Huxley quotes Lawrence as writing about himself, " 'Art for my sake' "; Huxley's comment on this is, I think, somewhat mistaken, for it ignores the driving concern of the later Lawrence: " . . . art, as he practiced it, and as, at the bottom, every artist, even the most pharisaically 'pure,' practices it, was 'art for my sake.' "

Both James and Lawrence seemed to be seeking at the ends of their lives a larger sort of commitment, a larger expression than pure self. If the artist really is condemned to repeat endlessly through his works, "Me, Me, Me," for Lawrence (and also for James) the true artist, the great artist, wants to say just as insistently, "Us, Us, Us." And it was to this effort that Lawrence devoted himself with all of his remaining strength in these last years.

If Lawrence's friend Richard Aldington is right, then all of Lawrence's work may be seen as a whole, as a "vast imaginative spiritual

---

[3]Compare this statement with the dying words of James' character Dencombe in "The Middle Years."

[4]In his introduction to Lawrence's *Apocalypse* (New York, 1932), xv.

autobiography."[4] The problem of ego-centrism in general and artistic ego-centrism in particular can be seen as a long continuous strand in this whole, stretching from the early *Sons and Lovers* in which the perils of obsessive selfhood are movingly depicted, through *Lady Chatterley's Lover* where the lovers gain a new kind of selfhood in their union, a kind of group identity, to the final *Apocalypse* in which Lawrence writes out of a new and liberated sense of the self and sees it as the Human Self in a vast cosmic perspective, freed from race, nationality, and even personality.

It is to this late period of the quest for a way to slough off the old skin of self and become a new Adam unsponsored and free that the short story "The Rocking-Horse Winner" belongs. The story means many things, of course, but surely one way to see it is in terms of this drive toward that greater, more generous concept of selfhood which I have noted. Seen in this context the story deals with the loss of ego-centric selfhood and the achievement of a new kind of selfhood based upon and instinct with the individual's sense of himself as a Human Being, a member of the race with all the limitations and ties and responsibilities which this implies — a Human Being aware of his relationship to all other Human Beings and aware also of the larger, over-arching relationship to the cosmos.

The progress of the story is outward from ego-centric selfhood as exemplified by Paul's relatives, each of them an isolated unit of tight introspection, and into a final, complete realization of self in which selfhood becomes selflessness. This is for Lawrence the apotheosis of selfhood and it is this which Paul achieves through death; if he cannot enjoy the benefits of this new state, surely we who have witnessed his sacrifice can. The death of Paul then is only a death to the kind of life led by his relatives who are themselves dead to all revelations, and it is at the same time symbolic of a rebirth to that greater, more generous, more permanent kind of selfhood. Paul dies happy because he has been released, and Lawrence makes this quite clear by titling the story "The Rocking-Horse *Winner*."

Most critics who have devoted serious attention to this story have been struck by the fabulistic tone of it. There is something stark, "primitive," echoic about the opening lines of the tale as though these were being uttered by a large, detached voice which was telling once again an ageless story. Yet though this tone has been noted by many, no one to my knowledge has thought it worthwhile to ask *why* it is that Lawrence should adopt such a tone. No one has asked whether the folkloric element might not have some thematic significance. In fact, it does have considerable thematic significance here, for it is through his use of traditions of the past that Lawrence illustrates his idea of new selfhood.

Beyond mere tone then the folkloric element is very strong indeed. A careful reading of the story and an awareness of folk motifs makes us aware that there are at least sixteen related motifs here and that the story as a whole bears interesting and important relationships to two related tale types.[5]

But this is not mere antiquarianism on Lawrence's part, nor is it a cheap attempt to lend to his fiction the dignity and weight that traditional art might confer. Instead, it is another manifestation of his long and serious interest in traditions and ways of thought of the far past. In part this interest is a natural by-product of Lawrence's view of himself as a visionary and as a writer of visionary literature, for it is an anthropological truism that the visionary finds the sources of his authority in the past rather than in the present where his enemies would deny the existence of any sources of inspiration (for if there were such, THEY would see them). But more importantly, this interest in traditions of the past, most particularly an interest in mythology, developed out of the artist's quest for true selfhood. It was in the age of myth and in the records of the myths themselves that Lawrence found that concept of self for which he had been searching.

The *locus classicus* for Lawrence on myth is a lengthy review of Frederick Carter's *The Dragon of the Apocalypse*, a review printed in the first volume of the posthumous papers. As in so much of his literary criticism, this review is more Lawrence than anybody else, and its speculations on the qualities of myth are distinctly his own, fired with that sense of urgency which characterizes the late writings. Myth, says Lawrence, is neither an argument, nor a parable. Instead,

> Myth is an attempt to narrate a whole human experience, of which the purpose is too deep, going too deep in the blood and soul, for mental explanation or description. We *can* expound the myth of Chronos very easily. We can explain it, we can even draw the moral conclusion. But we only look a little silly. The myth of Chronos lives beyond explanation, for it describes a profound experience of the human body and soul, an experience which is never exhausted, and which never will be exhausted, for it is

---

[5]The motifs I have reference to are to be found in Stith Thompson's *Motif-Index of Folk-Literature*, 6 vols. (Copenhagen and Bloomington, Ind., 1955-58), and are as follows: B542.2, B811.1, B184.1, B184.1.6, B141.2, B133, C762.3, D1620.2.1, D1626.1, F101.6.2, F159.2, F492, F66, J657.1, K985, R215.3. The tale types are to be found in A. Aarne and Stith Thompson, *The Types of the Folktale* (Helsinki, 1961), and are as follows: TT 313; TT 314.

being felt and suffered now, and will be felt and suffered while man remains man.[6]

This passage, it seems to me, does two important things: it warns against projecting the ego-centric self back into these ancient symbolic constructs (though this injunction does not stop Lawrence himself from using myths in a freely imaginative fashion), and it asks that we allow ourselves to be reborn through openly experiencing them. Lawrence is even more explicit about this latter possibility when he goes on to write:

> And the images of myth are symbols. They don't "mean something." They stand for units of human *feeling*, human experience. A complex of emotional experiences is a symbol. And the power of the symbol is to arouse the deep emotional self, the dynamic self, beyond comprehension. Many ages of accumulated experience still throb within a symbol, and we throb in response.

The deep, emotional self of which Lawrence writes here is that full sense of humanity, that true selfhood that he so eagerly sought in his last years and works, and for him the value of myth is that it can provide us with the means for an orgasmic release into true selfhood by transporting us back through time to that point in human history where man stood naked before the awful power and vast beauty of the universe and knew himself to be but Man. In *Apocalypse* Lawrence was to define precisely his view of the difference between men in the age of myth and men in the age of the machine:

> Perhaps the greatest difference between us and the pagans lies in our different relation to the cosmos. With us, all is personal. Landscape and sky, these are to us the delicious background of our personal life, and no more.
>
> To the pagan, landscape and personal background were on the whole indifferent. But the cosmos was a very real thing. A man *lived* with the cosmos, and knew it greater than himself.

This is the mysterious point toward which Paul rides his rocking-horse. " 'Well, I got there,' " Paul says to his uncomprehending mother, and when she asks where that might be, he can only reply, " 'Where I wanted to go.' " Where in fact that is has, I think, already been sufficiently indicated, but for emphasis we might look at one

---

[6]Edward D. McDonald (ed.), *Phoenix; The Posthumous Papers of D. H. Lawrence* (New York, 1936, 1968), pp. 295-296.

further passage from Lawrence's review of Carter's book on astral
mythology:

> To enter the astronomical sky of space is a great sensational
> experience. To enter the astrological sky of the zodiac and the
> living, roving planets is another experience, another *kind* of ex-
> perience; it is truly imaginative, and to me, more valuable. It is
> not the extension of what we already know: an extension which
> becomes awful, then appalling. *It is the entry into another world,*
> *another kind of world, measured by another dimension. And we*
> *find some prisoned self in us coming forth to live in this world.*
> (Italics in these last two sentences are mine.)

This then is what myth can do for us if we let it, and within the
myths themselves it is often the mythic hero on his quest who can
take us out of ourselves and by his sacrifice touch us deeply and at a
new level with the truth of our condition. This is how Paul functions
in "The Rocking-Horse Winner" — as a mythic hero whose quest
astride his horse takes us out of ourselves and whose sacrificial death
at the story's end might release us into that new sense of self which is
selflessness. In fact, this is the fate of all mythic heroes as Joseph
Campbell has made so clear:

> The hero . . . is the man or woman who has been able to battle
> past his personal and local historical limitations to the generally
> valid, normally human forms.[7]

More specifically, I suggest that "The Rocking-Horse Winner" is
built in part upon the myth of Bellerophon and his winged horse
Pegasus. Lawrence's use of this myth, however, is as freely interpretive
as we might expect, for in his view myths were always means and
never ends.

Central to both this myth and the short story is the figure of the
horse, an animal whose symbolic possibilities had long occupied the
writer's attention. From an early work *The Rainbow* (1915) through
to the essay on the Apocalypse, the horse "prances in to a purpose,"
often dark and inscrutable, and very often vaguely threatening. In my
view, the chief reason why the horse had such a hold on Lawrence's
imagination was that it had a similar one on the imaginations of
ancient men (as Lawrence himself remarked in the famous horse
passage in *Apocalypse*): the horse is perhaps next to the bear the
great animal of mythology. "Next to the human figure, the horse

---

[7]Joseph Campbell, *The Hero With a Thousand Faces* (New York, 1956), pp. 19-20.

appears as a favorite subject in all media of Greek art," writes Sidney Markman, and looking at those highly stylized bronze horses of 800 B.C., the majestic prancers of the Acropolis with their stiffly brushed manes, and that figure of the race horse found in the sea near Athens and dating from the middle of the Third Century B.C., his ears back, nostrils flaring, and delicate foreleg outthrust, one can fully believe this.[8] Here is Lawrence writing of the "old Greek horses" in *St. Mawr:*

> With their strangely naked equine heads, and something of a snake in their way of looking round, and lifting their sensitive, dangerous muzzles, they moved in a prehistoric twilight where all things loom phantasmagoric, all on one plane, sudden presences suddenly jutting out of the matrix. It was another world, an older, heavily potent world.

And when the heroine of that novel hears St. Mawr neigh,

> she seemed to hear echoes of another darker, more spacious, more dangerous, more splendid world than ours. . . .

This other world is the world of myth in which the consciousness of space is both that of the new sense of selfhood and of the vastness of the cosmos, the dimensionless aspect of eternity, and of Man's place in this whole. "Within the last fifty years," Lawrence writes in *Apocalypse,* "man has lost the horse. Now man is lost. Man is lost to life and power — an underling and a wastrel." It is the almost frenzied drive to return to that vibrant place in human history which goes far to explain the dark urgency of "The Rocking-Horse Winner."

In the story Paul's rocking-horse serves him (and hopefully the reader as well) in much the same way as Bellerophon's marvelous steed served him: to carry him away from the entanglements and deceits of this world toward a sphere of being in which the individual is freed of "the trash of personal feelings and ideas" (as Lawrence writes in *Apocalypse*). Paul, whom we may suppose to be as morbidly introspective as the rest of his relatives before his urgent quest on his magic horse, achieves his full humanity once he has dedicated himself to something larger than himself. This is precisely what the other characters in the story are unable to do, being as they are imprisoned within their ego-centric selves. Here once again we are reminded of the mythic associations of the horse and of what Lawrence made of these. Writing of the four horsemen of the Apocalypse, he finds them

---

[8]Sidney D. Markman, *The Horse in Greek Art* (Baltimore, 1943), p. 1.

obviously astrological, zodiacal, prancing in to a purpose. To what purpose? This time, really individual and human, rather than cosmic. The famous book of the seven seals in this place is the body of man: of a man: of Adam: of any man; and the seven seals are the seven centres or gates of his dynamic consciousness. We are witnessing the opening and conquest of the great psychic centres of the human body. The old Adam is going to be conquered, die, and be reborn as the new Adam.

The primal need of this old Adam here conquered is "to be, in his own sphere and as far as he can attain it, master, lord, and splendid one." The new Adam approximates in his new selfhood and cosmic consciousness those ancient men who lived so close to life itself that they could never forget what it was and what they were not. This quest for true selfhood and the conquest of the old ego-centric self is the hero's progress in myth and in "The Rocking-Horse Winner."

It may also be seen as the hero's progress in the tale types to which both Lawrence's short story and the classical myth of Bellerophon and Pegasus belong; these two tale types are grouped under the heading of "Magic Flight" and are composed of three major blocks of action: the severance of the boy from his natural surroundings; the forced performance by the hero of tasks, these involving in some way a magic horse; and the flight of the hero from his imprisonment. Seen in such skeletal fashion, it is clear how deeply indebted Lawrence was in the writing of this story to traditional art.

Both Bellerophon and Paul are exiled from their homelands: the mythic hero is sent from his native Corinth to Argos and from there to Lycia, bearing with him to this faraway Asian kingdom letters dictating his own destruction. So with Paul who is with his sisters exiled from the warm homeland of natural parental affection and understanding. The mother, Hester, cannot love anyone, perhaps because she loves herself far too much; and the father is so vague and distant a person that we are never told his name. So the boy becomes a sojourner in his own house, wandering aimlessly until the fading rocking-horse becomes his magic mount. Like Bellerophon, he vaults astride this marvelous animal and rides forth to conquests: Singhalese, Sansovino, Daffodil, Lively Spark — these are Paul's victories over the avarice, the destructive selfishness and neglect of his relatives; they are at the same time the psychological counterparts to Bellerophon's triumphs over the Chimaera, the Solymi warriors, and the Amazons.

But the conclusions of the classical myth and of Lawrence's short story are radically different, and it is this difference which defines in the clearest terms what the real object of Paul's quest is. In the myth

Bellerophon's final ride is the expression of excessive, unwarranted pride. In forgetting that it had been the gods, and particularly Athena, who had enabled him to catch and ride Pegasus to triumph, Bellerophon presumptuously attempts to ride the horse all the way to heaven — to become, in fact, one of the Olympians. But the gods are angered by this display of ego, and they cause the horse to throw his rider; he survives, it is true, but in such pitifully altered condition that he dies an obscure and ragged wanderer.

Paul's last ride is undertaken for entirely different reasons and is, in its own curious way, a triumphant ride. His victories in previous races have not served to assuage his parents' greed, for the whispers in the house have, under the stimulus of more money, burst forth "like a chorus of frogs on a spring evening." The money won is never an object for the mystic rider himself, a fact which Lawrence makes clear in a number of passages — the dialogue with the uncle in which Paul expresses his unwillingness to let his mother know that he is "lucky"; the boy's ready agreement that his mother should have the entire five thousand pounds; and his frantic desire to recoup for his parents the losses he has suffered on the Grand National and the Lincoln — all of which attest to his utter selflessness and perhaps also to his preternaturally acute feeling of pity for these adults so lost and walled up in their individual prisons.

Like Lawrence himself (and here the name Paul reminds us of the name of the intensely autobiographical hero of *Sons and Lovers* and reminds us further that these are the only two Lawrence characters so named), Paul must have known that to persist in his quest for "luck" would be to destroy himself. Even his Uncle Oscar, that handsome, smiling, empty-hearted man, urges him to " 'Let it alone,' " but the hero will not be dissuaded. Once again we recall Huxley's statement about Lawrence-as-artist: "His gift is his fate, and he follows a predestined course, from which no ordinary power can deflect him." It is not coincidental, I think, that Huxley's statement serves as a description of the mythic hero as well. And so Paul, the hero of this tale, cannot be swerved from his predestined course: he refuses to go away to the shore as his mother in vague concern wishes him to. In a dialogue which goes far to define the crucial spiritual differences between mother and son, the former is puzzled by her son's strong request that he not be sent away:

"Send you away from where? Just from this house?"
"Yes," he said, gazing at her.
"Why, you curious child, what makes you care about this house so much, suddenly? I never knew you loved it."
He gazed at her without speaking. He had a secret within a

secret, something he had not divulged, even to Bassett or to his Uncle Oscar.

What the child loves and cares about is, of course, not the house for which he has explicitly expressed hatred in an earlier conversation with his uncle, but instead his mother. This is his secret within a secret, and he will finally kill himself in behalf of her and his father and his uncle and the kind but passive Bassett. Unlike his mythic counterpart, Bellerophon, Paul's last ride is his penultimate expression of true selfhood, and in that final wild gallop he reaffirms his relationship with the dark, large forces of the cosmos. Lawrence's language in the final bedroom scene in which Paul is discovered in the midst of his midnight ride is heavily symbolic, almost Apocalyptic, one might say. Here is the mother listening to the noise from Paul's room:

> There was a strange, heavy, and yet not loud noise. Her heart stood still. It was a soundless noise, yet rushing and powerful. Something huge, in violent, hushed motion. What was it? What in God's name was it? She ought to know. She felt that she knew the noise. She knew what it was.
>
> Yet she could not place it. She couldn't say what it was.

In this climactic scene the mother hears the voice of the racial past, the voice of myth, calling in obscured words to her across the long stretches of time. It is the voice that her son has long since heard and responded to, but she cannot quite place it. She thinks that she ought to know what it is, and indeed she ought to, but she cannot finally place it. It is too late for her. She enters the room and switches on the light, flooding all in a sudden blaze. It is strongly reminiscent of that passage in the Apocalypse in which the visionary sees the heavens suddenly split apart and a white horse appear. Of this passage Lawrence was to write in his interpretation of *Revelation*:

> (The rider on the white horse) is my very me, my sacred ego, called into a new cycle ... and riding forth to conquest, the conquest of the old self for the birth of the new self. It is he, truly, who shall conquer all other "powers" of the self.

It is necessary, of course, to see Paul's death as this sort of achievement and triumph if this myth-centered reading of "The Rocking-Horse Winner" is to have much validity. Happily this requires no wrenching of art in the service of criticism, for Lawrence has shown in several places that death could indeed be looked upon as achievement and triumph provided the circumstances were right. Thus Lawrence on poetry and myth:

> Poetry is, as a rule, either the voice of the far future, exquisite and ethereal, or it is the voice of the past, rich, magnificent. When the Greeks heard the *Iliad* and the *Odyssey*, they heard their own past calling in their hearts, as men far inland sometimes hear the sea and fall weak with powerful, wonderful regret, nostalgia; or else their own future rippled its time-beats through their blood, as they followed the painful, glamorous progress of the Ithacan. This was Homer to the Greeks: their Past, splendid with battles won and *death achieved*, and their Future, the magic wandering of Ulysses through the unknown. (Italics mine)[9]

Death may be seen as an achievement if it is not an end in itself but rather *both* an end and a beginning of something better. Lawrence was prepared to see death in this fashion, for it is always the way in which it is seen in mythology: the deaths of heroes are the most important parts of their legends because they touch us profoundly with the sense of sacrifice and communal renewal. The hero becomes a hero only when he is willing to die in the service of others; thus he achieves both real selfhood and permanent herohood. As Coomaraswamy has said, " 'No creature can attain a higher grade of nature without ceasing to exist.' "[10]

So this death of the boy hero is but a death to a world populated with ego-maniacs like Paul's relatives, and it may be at the same time a rebirth for the audience which has witnessed this ultimate sacrifice.

Paul's final, orgasmic release into true selfhood and cosmic consciousness is achieved in his symbolic, sacrificial death; and Lawrence, as an artist always passionately concerned with the spiritual and emotional affects of his art upon his audience, must surely have intended this death to be a means toward our own liberation, toward the sloughing off of the old skins we wear and which make us so sadly interchangeable with the Hesters and nameless fathers and Oscar Creswells and well-meaning but sadly ineffectual Bassetts of this world. It may not be too great a stretch of the imagination to suggest that Lawrence was thinking not only of Bellerophon and Pegasus when he wrote this tale with its horses "prancing in to a purpose" and its heroic horseman as deliverer, but thinking also of *The Revelation*

---

[9]From the introduction to the American edition of *New Poems* (1918) in Vivian de Sola Pinto and Warren Roberts (eds.), *The Complete Poems of D. H. Lawrence* (New York, 1964), I, p. 181.

[10]Quoted by Campbell in *The Hero With a Thousand Faces*, p. 92.

to John. It is in *Revelation* that the idea of death as achievement is insisted upon in a more powerful way than in any other book of the New Testament. In *Revelation* 2:9 we read: "Be faithful unto death and I will give you the crown of life." And, "He who conquers shall not be hurt by the second death." It is then that first, that living death, which Paul conquers so that he does not "die" the second time. And it is his triumph, performed on a heroic scale worthy of a mythic figure, which might insure our own salvation.

Suggestions for Papers

Short Papers

Compare and contrast the interpretations of this story by Snodgrass and Turner.

Paul's mistaking "lucre" and "lucker" has been suggested as representing the essential confusion of values in the story. Is money made an object of worship?

Which of these essays speaks most convincingly to you about the story and why?

As substitutes for the "absent" father, what responsibility do Bassett and Uncle Oscar share in Paul's fate?

What positive values is Lawrence setting forth through this story?

What analogies, parallels, or similarities can you develop between the life here depicted and certain kinds of situations as you know of them or may have experienced?

Consider the elements of the "incredible" in the story and why they function successfully in spite of their being untrue to daily actuality.

Compare any situation, character, value, or stylistic element in this story with another story by Lawrence.

Paul's mother defines luck as "what causes you to have money." Obviously, Lawrence does not agree. What does he believe luck to be?

Bring your own perspective to bear on the points made by W. R. Martin in his article and the "Rebuttal" by W. D. Burroughs.

Consider the story from the standpoint of the way children "learn" the facts of the adult world — how they get their standards from adults.

Pursue the notion offered in the last page of the introduction which suggests that Bassett is the representative of a perverse "money-religion" by reading the poem "The Hound of Heaven," by the British poet Francis Thompson (1859-1907).

Long Papers

Choose one of the stories discussed by Frank Amon for a close comparative study with "The Rocking-Horse Winner."

Follow F. W. Turner's suggestion about similarities of theme between James' "The Pupil" and "The Rocking-Horse Winner" in an essay that points out the need for more consideration of the problem of Myth. One may, in a separate essay, point up and discuss the more than obvious differences between the stories.

Compare and contrast the relationship of Paul and his mother in the story with that of Paul Morel and his mother in *Sons and Lovers*.

Compare the effects of the mother-son relationship in the story with Lawrence's concepts of "education and sex" and "parental love" in his *Fantasia of the Unconscious*.

Compare the dramatic and thematic function of the horse in *St. Mawr* (published the same year, 1925) with that of the toy horse in the story.

Rewrite the story from a different point of view and in a subsequent page or two, discuss what the story gains or loses by such a change.

Compare the effects of the mother-son relationship in the story with Lawrence's ideas of proper upbringing in his *Psychoanalysis* and *the Unconscious*.

After reading Poe's story, "Ligeia," study Lawrence's essay on it in his *Studies in Classic American Literature*, comparing his attitudes on the destructive female with your own conception of Ligeia and Paul's mother.

Focusing on the theme of "sacrifice" as "punishment or redemption," compare the story with Hawthorne's "Roger Malvin's Burial."

Additional Readings

The best account of Lawrence criticism up to late 1958 has been checklisted by Maurice Beebe and Anthony Tommasi in *Modern Fiction Studies:* D. H. Lawrence Special Number, V, (Spring, 1959). Later entries can be found in F. W. Roberts' bibliography in the Soho Bibliographies series.

Arnold, Armin. *D. H. Lawrence and America.* London: Linden Press, 1958.

Bynner, Witter. *Journey with Genius: Recollections and Reflections Concerning The D. H. Lawrences.* New York: The John Day Company, Inc., 1951.

Chambers, Jessie. [E. T.] *D. H. Lawrence: A Personal Record.* London: Jonathan Cape, Ltd., 1935.

Daleski, H. M. *The Forked Flame.* Evanston: Northwestern University Press, 1965.

Draper, R. P. "D. H. Lawrence on Mother-Love," *Essays in Criticism,* VIII (July, 1958), 285-89.

Eliot, T. S. *After Strange Gods: A Primer of Modern Heresy.* New York: Harcourt, Brace & World, Inc., 1934.

Ford, George, H. Double Measure: *A Study of the Novels and Stories of D. H. Lawrence.* Holt, Rinehart & Winston, Inc., 1965.

Freeman, Mary. *D. H. Lawrence: A Basic Study of His Ideas.* Gainesville: University of Florida Press, 1955. Also New York: Grosset & Dunlap, The Universal Library, n.d.

Hoffman, Frederick J. and Harry T. Moore, editors. *The Achievement of D. H. Lawrence.* Norman: University of Oklahoma Press, 1953.

Hough, Graham. *The Dark Sun: A Study of D. H. Lawrence.* New York: The Macmillan Company, 1957.

Junkins, Donald, " 'The Rocking-Horse Winner': A Modern Myth," *Studies in Short Fiction,* II (Fall 1964), 87-88.

Lawrence, Frieda. *"Not I, But the Wind . . ."* New York: The Viking Press, Inc., 1934.

Leavis, F. R. *D. H. Lawrence: Novelist.* New York: Alfred A. Knopf, Inc., 1956.

Moore, Harry T. *The Life and Works of D. H. Lawrence.* New York: Twayne Publishers, Inc., 1951.

————. *The Intelligent Heart: The Story of D. H. Lawrence.* New York: Farrar, Straus & Young, 1954.

————. *The Collected Letters of D. H. Lawrence.* Two Volumes. New York: The Viking Press, Inc., 1962.

Moore, Harry T. and Warren Roberts. *D. H. Lawrence and His World.* New York: The Viking Press, Inc., 1966.

Moynahan, Julian. *The Deed of Life.* New Jersey: Princeton University Press, 1963.

Murry, John Middleton. *Son of Woman: The Story of D. H. Lawrence.* New York: Jonathan Cape and Harrison Smith, 1931.

Nin, Anais. *D. H. Lawrence: An Unprofessional Study.* Paris: Titus, 1932.

Sagar, Keith M. *The Art of D. H. Lawrence.* London: Cambridge University Press, 1966.

Spilka, Mark. *The Love Ethic of D. H. Lawrence.* Bloomington: Indiana University Press, 1955.

————, editor. *D. H. Lawrence: A Collection of Critical Essays.* New Jersey: Prentice-Hall, Inc., 1963.

Vivas, Eliseo. *D. H. Lawrence: The Failure and the Triumph of Art.* Evanston: Northwestern University Press, 1960.

Williams, Tennessee. "I Rise in Flame, Cried the Phoenix," *New World Writing* (April, 1952), 46-67.

Young, Kenneth. *D. H. Lawrence.* Writers and Their Work, No. 31. London: Longmans Green, 1952.

Glossary

ALLEGORY: A narrative or description in which characters, objects and events stand for a system of ideas, usually abstract, in a one-to-one ratio, item by item. Thus characters, objects and events are not important in themselves so much as the ideas they represent.

ATMOSPHERE: The general pervasive feeling aroused in the reader by various interrelating factors such as physical setting, time of year, weather, action, etc.

CLIMAX: The point at which the forces in conflict reach their highest peak, following which no further complication is usually involved and the denouement fairly imminent.

CONFLICT: Characters struggling against natural or social environment (external conflict); with conflicting forces in themselves (head *versus* heart); combinations and refinements of these. Determine the true center of conflict and you have taken an important step in the understanding of any story.

DENOUEMENT: The final resolution.

FORESHADOWING: The process of informing and preparing the reader through many means — direct exposition, repeated detail, a suggestive phrase — of some significant event to occur later in the story.

FORM: That which provides unity in a work of literature; the organization of ideas, images, characters, setting and the like to achieve a unifying effect. A story has achieved form when there is a functional relationship among these various elements, each contributing toward the intended effect. Form must *not* be thought of as a disposable container, a simple vehicle to convey idea, character and action. Any one of these may predominate, but form refers to the total principle of organization.

FUNCTIONAL: A term used in referring to elements that actually play a part in building up the complex and rich unity of a story. By contrast consider elements in less-than-quality or cheap fiction which are included merely because they are fashionable, decorative, or sensational.

IMAGERY: The representation in language of any sense experience. Mental picturing is merely one aspect of imagery; it may make an appeal to any of the senses: smell, sound, taste, and involve even texture, hardness and softness. Most common forms of imagery are in figurative language as *similes* or *metaphors*. A *simile* is a direct comparison between two things, introduced by *like* or *as*. A *metaphor* does not announce the comparison but identifies it, *i.e.* "his feet were clay."

INEVITABILITY: The sense that what results is the only possible result from the situation as previously given.

IRONY: A disparity between the anticipated and the actual, between appearance and reality, between an implied attitude and that actually stated. Some of the common forms of irony are: 1) *verbal* — a speaker says the opposite of what he means; 2) *dramatic* — a character is ignorant of his true situation of which the audience is aware; 3) *understatement* — the saying of less than the occasion warrants; and 4) irony of *situation* — disparity between the expected outcome of an action and the actual one.

MELODRAMATIC: When the violence or sensation is in excess of what the situation would seem to warrant in reference to motivation of character or to other elements in the story.

MOTIVATION: The purpose, or complex of purposes, drives, motives that determine the behavior of a character.

PARADOX: An apparent contradiction yet stating a truth, *i.e.* "to lie down in darkness and have your light in ashes."

PLOT: The sequence of events in time having a causal relationship; the structure of the action.

POINT OF VIEW: This phrase, applied to fiction, does *not* mean one's opinion or philosophical stance. A story must be narrated by someone, and point of view refers to the means of narration which basically are two: from *inside* the story, an "I" who participates in the story; or from *outside* the story, by the author. Further Distinctions:

1) Inside point of view: a) *first-person* — the narrator "I" telling the story is the main character;

                                     b) *first-person, witness* — the story concerns someone whom the narrator has observed, thus the "I" narrator is a minor character.

2) Outside point of view: a) *omniscient-author* — told in the third person, the author has full liberty (being god-like) to go into the minds of characters and to give his own comment;

                                       b) *limited-omniscient* or *objective-author* — again the story is told in the third person but the author restricts his omniscience to one character; and/or concentrates on observed elements: deeds, words, gestures and withholds his own comment.

REALISTIC: Having a strong sense of verisimilitude, fact or actuality, thus creating the illusion of life as lived.

SENTIMENTALITY: An action or description involving an emotional response in excess of the occasion.

SYMBOL: An object, character, or incident generally significant in its own right, but having a range of meaning beyond itself.

SETTING: The environment—physical, temporal, and social—in which a story takes place.

TONE: The author's attitude toward his material, conveyed mainly in the choice of and pattern of words that reveal his own feelings about the situations or characters, *i.e.* satiric, sardonic, comic, etc.

THEME: In a work of fiction the guiding or controlling idea which that fiction dramatizes or illustrates: "What is the point of this story?"

General Instructions
For A Research Paper

If your instructor gives you any specific directions about the format of your research paper that differ from the directions given here, you are, of course, to follow his directions. Otherwise, you can observe these directions with the confidence that they represent fairly standard conventions.

A research paper represents a student's synthesis of his reading in a number of primary and secondary works, with an indication, in footnotes, of the source of quotations used in the paper or of facts cited in paraphrased material. A *primary* source is the text of a work as it issued from the pen of the author or some document contemporary with the work. The following, for instance, would be considered primary sources: a manuscript copy of the work; first editions of the work and any subsequent editions authorized by the writer; a modern scholarly edition of the text; an author's comment about his work in letters, memoirs, diaries, journals, or periodicals; published comments on the work by the author's contemporaries. A *secondary* source would be any interpretation, explication, or evaluation of the work printed, usually several years after the author's death, in critical articles and books, in literary histories, and in biographies of the author. In this casebook, the text of the work, any variant versions of it, any commentary on the work by the author himself or his contemporaries may be considered as primary sources; the editor's Introduction, the articles from journals, and the excerpts from books are to be considered secondary sources. The paper that you eventually write will become a secondary source.

Plagiarism

The cardinal sin in the academic community is plagiarism. The rankest form of plagiarism is the verbatim reproduction of someone else's words without any indication that the passage is a quotation. A lesser but still serious form of plagiarism is to report, in your own words, the fruits of someone else's research without acknowledging the source of your information or interpretation.

You can take this as an inflexible rule: every verbatim quotation in your paper must be either enclosed in quotation marks or single-spaced and inset from the left-hand margin and must be followed by a footnote number. Students who merely change a few words or phrases in a quotation and present the passage as their own work are still guilty of plagiarism. Passages of genuine paraphrase must be footnoted too if the information or idea or interpretation contained in the paraphrase cannot be presumed to be known by ordinary educated people or at least by readers who would be interested in the subject you are writing about.

The penalties for plagiarism are usually very severe. Don't run the risk of a failing grade on the paper or even of a failing grade in the course.

Lead-Ins

Provide a lead-in for all quotations. Failure to do so results in a serious breakdown in coherence. The lead-in should at least name the person who is being quoted. The ideal lead-in, however, is one that not only names the person but indicates the pertinence of the quotation.

Examples:

> (typical lead-in for a single-spaced, inset quotation)

> Irving Babbitt makes this observation about
> Flaubert's attitude toward women:

(typical lead-in for quotation worked into the frame of one's sentence)

> Thus the poet sets out to show how the present
> age, as George Anderson puts it, "negates the
> values of the earlier revolution."[7]

Full Names

The first time you mention anyone in a paper give the full name of the person. Subsequently you may refer to him by his last name.

Examples: First allusion—Ronald S. Crane
                 Subsequent allusions—Professor Crane,
                 as Crane says.

Ellipses

Lacunae in a direct quotation are indicated with *three spaced periods,* in addition to whatever punctuation mark was in the text at the point where you truncated the quotation. *Hit the space-bar of your typewriter between each period.* Usually there is no need to put the ellipsis-periods at the beginning or the end of a quotation.

Example: "The poets were not striving to communicate with their audience; . . . By and large, the Romantics were seeking . . . to express their unique personalities."[8]

Brackets

Brackets are used to enclose any material interpolated into a direct quotation. The abbreviation *sic,* enclosed in brackets, indicates that the error of spelling, grammar, or fact in a direct quotation has been copied as it was in the source being quoted. If your typewriter does not have special keys for brackets, draw the brackets neatly with a pen.

Examples: "He [Theodore Baum] maintained that Confucianism [the primary element in Chinese philosophy] aimed at teaching each individual to accept his lot in life."[12]

"Paul Revear [sic] made his historic ride on April 18, 1875 [sic]."[15]

Summary Footnote

A footnote number at the end of a sentence which is not enclosed in quotation marks indicates that only *that* sentence is being documented in the footnote. If you want to indicate that the footnote documents more than one sentence, put a footnote number at the end of the *first* sentence of the paraphrased passage and use some formula like this in the footnote:

[16] For the information presented in this and the following paragraph, I am indebted to Marvin Magalaner, Time of Apprenticeship: the Fiction of Young James Joyce (London, 1959), pp. 81-93.

Citing the Edition

The edition of the author's work being used in a paper should always be cited in the first footnote that documents a quotation from that work. You can obviate the need for subsequent footnotes to that edition by using some formula like this:

⁴ Nathaniel Hawthorne, "Young Goodman Brown," as printed in Young Goodman Brown, ed. Thomas E. Connolly, Charles E. Merrill Literary Casebooks (Columbus, Ohio, 1968), pp. 3-15. This edition will be used throughout the paper, and hereafter all quotations from this book will be documented with a page-number in parentheses at the end of the quotation.

Notetaking

Although all the material you use in your paper may be contained in this casebook, you will find it easier to organize your paper if you work from notes written on 3 x 5 or 4 x 6 cards. Besides, you should get practice in the kind of notetaking you will have to do for other term-papers, when you will have to work from books and articles in, or on loan from, the library.

An ideal note is a self-contained note—one which has all the information you would need if you used anything from that note in your paper. A note will be self-contained if it carries the following information:

(1) The information or quotation *accurately* copied.

(2) Some system for distinguishing direct quotation from paraphrase.

(3) All the bibliographical information necessary for documenting that note—full name of the author, title, volume number (if any), place of publication, publisher, publication date, page numbers.

(4) If a question covered more than one page in the source, the note-card should indicate which part of the quotation occurred on one page and which part occurred on the next page. The easiest way to do this is to put the next page number in parentheses after the last word on one page and before the first word on the next page.

In short, your note should be so complete that you would never have to go back to the original source to gather any piece of information about that note.

Footnote Forms

The footnote forms used here follow the conventions set forth in the *MLA Style Sheet*, Revised Edition, ed. William Riley Parker, which is now used by more than 100 journals and more than thirty university presses in the United States. Copies of this pamphlet can be purchased for fifty cents from your university bookstore or from the Modern Language Association, 62 Fifth Avenue, New York, N.Y. 10011. If your teacher or your institution prescribes a modified form of this footnoting system, you should, of course, follow that system.

A primary footnote, the form used the first time a source is cited, supplies four pieces of information: (1) author's name, (2) title of the source, (3) publication information, (4) specific location in the source of the information or quotation. A secondary footnote is the shorthand form of documentation after the source has been cited in full the first time.

Your instructor may permit you to put all your footnotes on separate pages at the end of your paper. But he may want to give you practice in putting footnotes at the bottom of the page. Whether the footnotes are put at the end of the paper or at the bottom of the page, they should observe this format of spacing: (1) the first line of each footnote should be indented, usually the same number of spaces as your paragraph indentations; (2) all subsequent lines of the footnote should start at the lefthand margin; (3) there should be single-spacing within each footnote and double-spacing between each footnote.

Example:

[10] Ruth Wallerstein, Richard Crashaw: A Study in Style and Poetic Development, University of Wisconsin Studies in Language and Literature, No. 37 (Madison, 1935), p. 52.

Primary Footnotes

(The form to be used the *first* time a work is cited)

[1] Paull F. Baum, Ten Studies in the Poetry of Matthew Arnold (Durham, N.C., 1958), p. 37.
   (book by a single author; p. is the abbreviation of *page*)

[2] René Wellek and Austin Warren, Theory of Literature (New York, 1949), pp. 106-7.
   (book by two authors; pp. is the abbreviation of *pages*)

³ William Hickling Prescott, <u>History</u> <u>of</u> <u>the</u> <u>Reign</u>
<u>of</u> <u>Philip</u> <u>the</u> <u>Second,</u> <u>King</u> <u>of</u> <u>Spain,</u> ed. John Foster
Kirk (Philadelphia, 1871), II, 47.

(an edited work of more than one volume; *ed.* is the abbreviation
for "edited by"; note that whenever a volume number is cited, the
abbreviation p. or pp. is *not* used in front of the page number)

⁴ John Pick, ed., <u>The</u> <u>Windhover</u> (Columbus, Ohio
1968), p. 4.

(form for quotation from an editor's Introduction—as, for instance,
in this casebook series; here *ed.* is the abbreviation for "editor")

⁵ A.S.P. Woodhouse, "Nature and Grace in <u>The</u> <u>Faerie</u>
<u>Queen,</u>" in <u>Elizabethan</u> <u>Poetry</u>: <u>Modern</u> <u>Essays</u> <u>in</u>
<u>Criticism</u>, ed. Paul J. Alpers (New York, 1967),
pp. 346-7.

       (chapter or article from an edited collection)

⁶ Morton D. Paley, "Tyger of Wrath," <u>PMLA</u>, LXXXI
(December, 1966), 544.

(an article from a periodical; note that because the volume number
is cited no p. or pp. precedes the page number; the titles of periodicals are often abbreviated in footnotes but are spelled out in the
Bibliography; here, for instance, *PMLA* is the abbreviation for
Publications of the Modern Language Association)

Secondary Footnotes

(Abbreviated footnote forms to be used after a work has been cited
once in full)

⁷ Baum, p. 45.
(abbreviated form for work cited in footnote #1; note that the
secondary footnote is indented the same number of spaces as the
first line of primary footnotes)

⁸ Wellek and Warren, pp. 239-40.
      (abbreviated form for work cited in footnote #2)

⁹ Prescott, II, 239.
  (abbreviated form for work cited in footnote #3; because this is
a multi-volume work, the volume number must be given in addition to the page number)

¹⁰ <u>Ibid</u>., p. 245.
(refers to the immediately preceding footnote—that is, to page
245 in the second volume of Prescott's history; *ibid.* is the abbre-

viation of the Latin adverb *ibidem* meaning "in the same place"; note that this abbreviation is italicized or underlined and that it is followed by a period, because it is an abbreviation)

[11] Ibid., III, 103.

(refers to the immediately preceding footnote—that is, to Prescott's work again; there must be added to *ibid.* only what changes from the preceding footnote; here the volume and page changed; note that there is no p. before 103, because a volume number was cited)

[12] Baum, pp. 47-50.

(refers to the same work cited in footnote #7 and ultimately to the work cited in full in footnote #1)

[13] Paley, p. 547.

(refers to the article cited in footnote #6)

[14] Rebecca P. Parkin, "Mythopoeic Activity in the Rape of the Lock," ELH, XXI (March, 1954), 32.

(since this article from the *Journal of English Literary History* has not been previously cited in full, it must be given in full here)

[15] Ibid., pp. 33-4.

(refers to Parkin's article in the immediately preceding footnote)

Bibliography Forms

Note carefully the differences in bibliography forms from footnote forms: (1) the last name of the author is given first, since bibliography items are arranged alphabetically according to the surname of the author (in the case of two or more authors of a work, only the name of the first author is reversed); (2) the first line of each bibliography item starts at the lefthand margin; subsequent lines are indented; (3) periods are used instead of commas, and parentheses do not enclose publication information; (4) the publisher is given in addition to the place of publication; (5) the first and last pages of articles and chapters are given; (6) most of the abbreviations used in footnotes are avoided in the Bibliography.

The items are arranged here alphabetically as they would appear in the Bibliography of your paper.

Baum, Paull F. Ten Studies in the Poetry of Matthew
    Arnold. Durham, N.C.: University of North
    Carolina Press, 1958.

Paley, Morton D. "Tyger of Wrath," Publications of the Modern Language Association, LXXXI (December, 1966), 540-51.

Parkin, Rebecca P. "Mythopoeic Activity in the Rape of the Lock," Journal of English Literary History, XXI (March, 1954), 30-8.

Pick, John, editor. The Windhover. Columbus, Ohio: Charles E. Merrill Publishing Company, 1968.

Prescott, William Hickling. History of the Reign of Philip the Second, King of Spain. Edited by John Foster Kirk. 3 volumes. Philadelphia: J.B. Lippincott and Company, 1871.

Wellek, René and Austin Warren. Theory of Literature. New York: Harcourt, Brace & World, Inc., 1949.

Woodhouse, A.S.P. "Nature and Grace in The Faerie Queene," in Elizabethan Poetry: Modern Essays in Criticism. Edited by Paul J. Alpers. New York: Oxford University Press, 1967, pp. 345-79.

If the form for some work that you are using in your paper is not given in these samples of footnote and bibliography entries, ask your instructor for advice as to the proper form.